The House of Dragonflies

SMITHA MENON KIZHUVEETIL

Clever Fox® PUBLISHING

Chennai • Bangalore

CLEVER FOX PUBLISHING
Chennai, India

Published by CLEVER FOX PUBLISHING 2025

Editor: Tanmay Dubey

ISBN: 978-93-6707-262-2

TO THE MOTHER IN YOU

For Shivamsh, the morning in my every story…

CONTENTS

ACKNOWLEDGEMENTS

I pay homage to the few objects and mental images that set me on this journey last summer. Some of them are the sound of the uniquely huge and heavy elephant chain that's kept as a monument in the eastern entrance of Koodalmanikyam Temple, the sight of a fallen tree, the touch of a one-eyed doll, the smile of a lost playmate, the silence of an attic and so on. These have stayed with me continuously, spurring my interest ever since childhood. They took me to reimagine a few chapters in some lives I have seen, I have heard and known.

My deep reverence to my grandparents, parents, uncles and aunts. Some have been compelling narrators whose oral sagas I have been fortunate enough to listen to. The conversations I had with my father, V Peethambaran, and my uncle, V Radhakrishnan, before my first word made its way onto the pages of this novel, awakened my enthusiasm for writing, and I sincerely thank them for that. I am also grateful to my mother, K Lalitha, who always bought me books, and to my uncle, K Viswanathan, for his small bookshelf during my younger days. They introduced me to the wonderful world of reading.

I sincerely acknowledge the divine interactions with myself, my characters and the utterly unanticipated ones with a few strangers who left me with food for thought. Their support in scaffolding the narrative is immense, especially at its crucial junctures and turns. I thank Karnan (Madurai), Mani Kannan (Thanjavur), Chandrasekharan Nambiar (Mayiladuthurai), A. Christable (Chennai), Perumal E (Tambaram), and Ms Jenusha K S (Department of Archaeology, Maharaja's College, Ernakulam, 2023-2024).

I extend genuine appreciation to my book-writing coach, mentor, and editor, author Tanmay Dubey, for his steady guidance throughout. He helped me dispel my doubts and free myself from moments of skepticism with a gentle nudge forward in the right direction during this creative undertaking. To be specific, his words "*Just write on...*" got me the impetus to turn this possibility into reality.

Many thanks to the entire team at Clever Fox Publishing for bringing this piece to life.

I have a great deal of admiration for the writers Dr Pushpangadan Mangari, Manoj Menon and E. Prabhakaran Nair for their unwavering support and heartening comments.

Thank you, the staff of the Archaeological Survey of India (ASI), Thrissur, Dr. Sheena Anil, Dr. Pradeepkumar T D, Dr. Fiju Chacko, Dr. Sam P J and Dr. Anju Tresa Andrews, for your patient and invaluable sessions addressing my queries.

Grateful beyond words to my family, friends, colleagues, and students for your continued encouragement.

My most humble and boundless love for everything that lent me insight, inspiration and support along this path of creation. And finally, this book is dedicated to the people of my blood and beyond, whose emotional presence I often feel. Some were gone, some are lost. I consider them miracles like the rain that wraps, like the river that flows and leaves for its true abode - the Ocean of miracles.

"Every story is us."

– Rumi

CHAPTER 1

THE REVISIT

29 June 2024

Viruthi, a quaint village in mid-Kerala, is always vibrant and has a bounteous nature. But once the aroma of petrichor settles in after the rain, the village would shudder awake, uniquely summoning forth the long-buried greenness from the summer's tomb. The narrow passageways of the village are all interconnected and eventually converge at the Viruthiyaru (River Viruthi). It was the onset of monsoon, and the jubilant June decorated both the village and the river with its spectacular brilliance. The river's mellifluous flow, touching both banks, lured visitors from far-off places.

A Tata Tiago sped across the old bridge, its tyres humming against the worn surface. It swerved gently towards the causeway that ran parallel to the river. The old stone wall, built during the pre-independence days, rose and stretched along like a silent witness to time. Once narrow and clay-streaked, it had been widened and tarred over the years, its jagged edges now softened by decades of weathering.

The overcast sky and dark verdure further dimmed the terrain. Dozens of concrete houses with small courtyards and plantations lined the sidewalks. Some of the area on the other side of the way, by the river, had been reclaimed by water.

The vehicle came to a halt in front of a narrow gravel path. It led up to a desolate region where thickets grew abundantly. Charulatha, a medium-built, dusky woman in her forties, wearing a green *sari,* stepped out of the car. Her unkempt curly hair had a hint of grey. A deep dimple appeared on her left cheek as her fingers nimbly attempted to tame some rebellious strands. The woman's uncolored amber-brown eyes framed her face with an enigmatic halo that seemed to glow as she moved through the premises.

The day was young, and in the mellow light, she saw the house as a forsaken statement of the past. A stream of past memories passed through her eyes, and she remained intoxicated as if she had consumed some potion.

The house was bare, like the body evicted from its soul. Once a sturdy building that contributed to nurturing lives, it remained a reflection. Charulatha scooped up the soil under her feet and brought it close to her forehead. It was swampy after the monsoon rain.

The smell of damp earth!

She stood gazing upward. The same little girl was looking at her, from there, perhaps with the same innocence, through the dusty corners of the attic. She felt.

The bustling wildlife and lush foliage had retaken the surroundings. The site held a canvas with bursts of colour. The mossy soil resembled a green lagoon upon which smiled the little tree plants caparisoned with their tiny suns. Petite wildflowers peeked through the cracks in the pavement. Butterflies fluttered and flitted around, their delicate wings creating a kaleidoscopic display. A scurry of squirrels hurried up a nearby tree. Their bushy tails added a touch of festivity to the serene scene. They wavered like the sacred fly whisks in a row, eventually making the branches sprinkle the guttated water on the lady.

A soft gale with an enticing fragrance came from the pond below the grove. She caught a glimpse of a majestic peacock with its lustrous plumage shimmering in the sunlight.

'How come peacocks are here! Never did they show up back then!' She thought.

The woman remained contemplative. The captivating tapestry of nature entwined with the vestiges of the past created wistful sighs in her heart.

She took out a cold iron key from her bag and stepped closer to the weathered building. The old teak double doors stood resolutely shut in front of her. The key she inserted into the rusted keyhole seemed reluctant to fit. After several attempts, the heavy doors swung open with a loud creak, revealing the dimly lit interior. Her footfall made the old floorboards groan in protest. The walls, worn and decayed, and the moth-eaten wooden roof whispered tales of forgotten years, pulling her back to a time when she was a young girl, full of innocence and freedom. The distant echoes of many mothers' voices lingered in the air, calling her name. Charulatha responded, her heart swelling as the gentle, comforting sounds enveloped her, wrapping her in a cocoon of warmth and love.

She walked past the house, aiming at the southwest corner. The area was shrouded in the debris of a caved-in well and some concrete slabs. Dragonflies flew up and down above the well. She looked down into it to see an image masked by the dense vegetation.

'Where am I?' A voice in her mind asked.

She was transfixed. With a sigh, she looked up, but her vision was blurred by uninvited tears.

Something magnificent began to emerge before her. It was a spreader of comfy companionship. It stretched out its branches, sieving sunlight to the rain-kissed earth. Like an eternal light that casts all evils out. In a splash of emotions, she embraced the tree trunk which was visible only to her. Something irresistible resonated within the lady, a call to merge into the subtlest forms that existed once. It was never like her feelings, which used to be slumped in a cluttered mind. A sort of serenity whirled her. Tears started streaming down.

"I am back in your arms. Hold me."

She continued mumbling until she felt a chill around her left foot. A shiver ran down her spine. The strength that held suddenly evanesced. She gazed down to see a sleek creature slowly slithering from the rubble. Its scaly body glinted like some strange ornament.

As it inched forward, she couldn't help but feel a strange connection to the creature. The reptile abruptly halted as if it had sensed something familiar. It raised its hood and turned to her, bound by a charismatic spell from her. Its cold eyes seemed to reflect her inner struggles and fears, an impression of Charulatha.

Her eyes kept trailing its path. The serpent resumed its retrieval at the *Kavu* (*Sarpa Kavu* or the Sacred Serpent Grove) a few yards away from the well. The grove was amidst the bamboo thickets and enormous trees. The encounter left her both unsettled and intrigued as if it held a deeper meaning that she unravelled. She was surprisingly calm and stood with a greater proclivity for everything around.

Charulatha pursued the snake. She struggled not to disturb the touch-me-nots, and they seemed to reciprocate with careful reverence. The west of the vicinity was mostly a canopy of wild creepers and massive trees. They stood as sentries of time, welcoming her. The wild hibiscus, ixora, and the royal red pagoda flowers were seen in profusion along the track. Towering trees loomed larger with their gnarled branches draped by countless bats in eerie clusters. The rustling of their wings and the occasional piercing screech amplified the scary atmosphere.

Charulatha, 'the beautiful creeper', as she was once called by her Achamma (paternal grandmother), unfalteringly entered the *Kavu*, the custodian of tradition and faith. She cleaned the raised stony platform, wet amidst the grove, removing the fallen leaves and dust. The platform, once hidden under neglect, now gleamed under the gentle touch of her care. Her hands reached into her handbag, retrieving a small oil lamp and a matchbox. She fired it to light the lamp with utmost devotion and stood with folded hands. Charulatha was like a drop of nectar drawn to the folds of a dark flower. She remained there for many seconds and strolled towards the pond, *Kalikulam*, below the edge.

"Don't go to the pond."

An unexpected command fell into her ears.

She turned to see a lean, bare-chested man in his thirties. He seemed inquisitive about the strange visitor early in the day.

"No one uses the pond. That west corner is *Kalikavu*. No one should go there. Besides, the boulders are loose and slippery."

He continued with a sceptical tone.

"Nobody enters here. Who are you? Not even the blood relations visit Chittezham. Two months back, some college students came to have their escapades here. It's too annoying to see people disturb this place."

Charulatha felt happy to hear him, who sounded protective of the soil. But the word 'blood' choked her. She wanted to declare to the world that she was the blood and that she belonged to the soil, but something held her back, making her silent.

"There is no treasure here." The man sneered.

"For me, there." The woman broke her silence.

He stood curious at her remark and said with a grin. "Maybe you would get corpses, sister."

From him, Charulatha heard that there was no human settlement around the area. No one in the bloodline remained. Humans dreaded the place like a nightmare. Children were never allowed to collect flowers from the land during the *Onam* (the annual harvest festival celebrated by the people of Kerala) season. The locals wouldn't even let their cattle graze there.

According to local belief, the place had been cursed and haunted. On new moon nights, the land transformed into a graveyard where children's cries would be heard. Even a blade of grass there would be poisonous. No residents were left there.

After the flood in 2018, there were no walls to separate Chittezham from its surroundings. It was widely open, with its wild serpentine charm. People became enamoured with the land. But no one dared to enter the premises except miscreants.

The man came closer to her and whispered in a mysterious vein.

"Are you here to write stories or create reels?" The man laughed.

"Don't get enchanted. You will be trapped."

Charulatha moved a step back, and behind her, the lamp flickered in the breeze. It was then he noticed the lamp on the altar.

"Did you light that?"

The man was surprised to hear her.

" Yes. I belong here.."

He seemed urged to ask her something further, but he stopped with a shadow of uneasiness on his face. He didn't feel fine being with the family's blood anymore and left the place hastily.

The woman stood calm and then broke her reverie and began walking towards the pond. It lay just below the edge of the serpent grove at the western extremity, marked by massive bamboo thickets. The terrain, along with the pond, used to be the most dreaded place known as *Kalikavu*, which the locals also referred to as *Kalikulam*.

The pond resembled a brimming container, merrily filled by the season with its verdant wine. Its surface was festooned with wildflowers, like starlets. Charulatha breathed with her full passion to savor its delicious fragrance. A child was reborn in her. She smiled a smile that was unmindful of all anguishes in the world. With a soulful reverence, she gazed skyward and then peered into the pond's depths. She took out something from her bag and stretched out her palm. It was a *chembakam* (*Champa* flower). She placed the flower on a step that led to the water.

Charulatha was back at her ancestral home after one and a half decades. The land held an array of inexhaustible tales waiting to be exhumed. Her mind roamed as if traversing the cherished hallways of her childhood memories. That little universe created by endless love and countless stories. With each step, Charulatha became an unusual collocation with the long-gone sensations. She finally found herself. The humid air received her sighs drenched in joyful tears.

❖ ❖ ❖

CHAPTER 2

DAUGHTERS OF THE DUSK

4 July 2024

Thiruvananthapuram

'The colour of our souls is that of their wings, daughter. Souls reside in them in subtle and translucent form. They are as pure as tears. How clear, transparent, and light, aren't they? They visit the purest places...'

Tonight, I feel them buzzing over me as I pen this...the story of a dreaded land.

The story of my house, my village, and my river. And therefore, it's Charulatha's story too. Story of Charulatha Chittezham.

❖ ❖ ❖

Chittezham, was a notable *Nair* (one of the *Hindu* castes in Kerala) family that held a prominent position in the village of Viruthi. The early residents of the house bore the pedigree of *the Namboothiris, also known as Kerala Brahmins*. Over the years, generations had enjoyed its opulent aristocratic standards hugely. But with time, its grandeur dwindled. Frequent lashes of adversity brought its abysmal fall.

All began with the darkest shadow lurking beneath the surface, threatening to disrupt the simple paradise there. The Chittezham family, once respected and revered, along with the village of Viruthi harboured a sinister twist of fate that altered everything.

Many moons ago, long before the separation between the village and the river came, Viruthiyaru was wider and used to flow much more adjacent to the Chittezham land, creating some inlets. The occupants on the left of the river were upper castes. It was an amazingly prosperous land, known for its plenteous harvests, thriving economy, flourishing community, and cattle. It was before the system *Marumakkathayam* (The system in *Nair Tharavad* where matriarchy was practised. The girl born into the family would be given a higher role and power) came into practice.

Chittezham Chandran Nair, the youngest son of the *Karanavar* (addressing the head of the family), married a beautiful girl named Kunjikkavu of the Koroth family. She was a simple, innocent, compassionate girl of high virtue and was sincerely devoted to her husband Chandran Nair.

The couple didn't have children. Kunjikkavu was an ardent devotee of the serpent gods and her prayers and entreaties to them at the Chittezham *Kavu* were finally heard. She became pregnant. It was towards the end of the *Malayalam* month, *Karkkadakam* (*Malayalam* is the language spoken by people of Kerala); when her date was due, Kunjikkavu witnessed something in her chamber that she least expected. She saw her husband in a coital embrace with a woman of his distant relation. Kunjikkavu collapsed and with that, she lost the baby. She went mute after the incident. The trauma she consumed that night remained unabated, and the poor woman lost her mind.

It was creepy to see Kunjikkavu roaming inside the *Kavu*, sometimes whining and sometimes laughing. At the peak of her frenzied mood, she used to swirl around the areca nut palms incessantly, her giggles accompanying her. Nobody realised the reason for her derangement other than her husband.

Chandran Nair never felt remorseful, instead, he began taunting Kunjikkavu. Simultaneously, his love galas doubled day by day. The whole village lamented Chandran Nair's plight of having a crazy consort and everybody assumed that some evil spirit had possessed Kunjikkavu. The mad woman was not even accepted at her own home. The siblings of Kunjikkavu were not willing to take her back due to their poverty.

Chandran Nair's relatives took her to Chottanikkara Temple hoping to dispel the evil in her. She was put in fetters there for many months. Kunjikkavu suffered alone for no fault of her own. Once a female *sadhu* accosted her. She touched Kunjikkavu's forehead with some incantations and bequeathed her with an amulet. Kunjikkavu started showing gradual changes after the incident and was later returned to Chittezham.

By then, Chandran Nair married another woman. Kunjikkavu's position at Chittezham was worse than that of a slave. Years passed. Chandran Nair fathered half a dozen children with his second wife. Kunjikkavu never claimed her husband back. She lived in complete destitution. What she owned was her *Thali* (the nuptial locket) and the amulet she always wore.

She became a wilted flower, drawing inward. The shine had left her eyes, and she grew complacent about everything around her. Yet, amidst all her miseries, she never ceased to worship the serpent gods. Surprisingly, as the days passed, some invisible powers seemed to grow around Kunjikkavu.

The only human connection surging within her was for her lost baby. At times, the sorrowful mother pined before the unseen gods. She didn't know where her baby had been buried. All her hope resided at the river and *Kavu*. She languished there for many years, and her mournful sighs were likely to disrupt the ecosystem of Chittezham.

Kunjikkavu was in the grip of extreme pain, and she adopted harsher measures to scourge herself. She began fasting and doing penance by the *Kavu*, unbeknownst to the family members. With time, she became a symbol of undaunted courage.

On new moon nights, she visited the *Kavu* with a lantern in her hand, stared into its darkness for hours, and then immersed herself in the river. The depths of the darkest skies and the waters equally tranquilised her. It's rumoured that Kunjikkavu had learned the language of the elements and used it to communicate with the creatures around them.

On one such occasion, at the seventh hour of a new moon night, Kunjikkavu heard something from the red hibiscus bushes after her nocturnal ablution in the river. In the lantern's dim light, she caught sight of a gleaming form of a black cobra. A baby girl was found in the mud, fully wrapped in the muddy water. A golden aura emanated from the baby.

With Kunjikkavu's approach, the serpent slowly disappeared into the grove. As she held the baby, 'the mother' in her, burst into tears. Her breasts were wet with the tender lullabies of her heart. Unlike the newborns, the baby was too dark.

The overjoyed Kunjikkavu considered the baby to be goddess *Kali's* boon. It was as if she had been waiting for this strange meeting. She cleaned the baby with her *kachamundu* (cotton bath towel), and with a gracious smile, she gently whispered 'Kunjikkali' in her ears. A gentle breeze swept over the bushes, carrying with it the sweet fragrance of *chembakam* (flower *champa*). Kunjikkavu wondered at the waft, as no Champa tree was on the premises. She felt the baby close to her again and again. She smelled like the flower!

The weirdest fact about the girl was that she lacked an umbilicus. The story of the mysterious child spread across the village like wildfire. The queer origin of the girl and her bizarre features dreaded everybody. Though in the beginning, the girl grew up at Chittezham she was never welcomed by the family. But, since they sensed the powers that Kunjikkavu developed along with the amulet, they feared shunning both of them.

They raised a hut near the river and isolated the girl and her mother. The little girl grew faster. She was a shadow of her foster mother. She accompanied Kunjikkavu in all her chores. The girl was fond of cattle and was often seen in their company. Kunjikkavu never lost her steadfastness. She had unwavering faith in the serpent gods and goddess *Kali* and pursued her silent acts by the river.

Gods could be black, but never humans. Kunjikkali's charismatic sheen could entice people. Still, she was untouchable to all, and so became her foster mother, Kunjikkavu. The family expected them to starve and perish in isolation. But the mother and daughter never gave up. The fiendish motives of the Chittezham family never succeeded.

Kunjikkavu recuperated with time. Her changed stance and mental fortitude bewildered others. They wanted to destroy the grove, obliterating the very existence of the mother and the child. For the first time, Kunjikkavu stood as a formidable barrier in front of them, not allowing them to commit the vile act.

Soon the family members fell into the grip of the deadliest contagion. Gradually, each member yielded to the inevitable. The disease spread far and wide, sweeping off numerous lives.

The village chief was alarmed. Elderly men sat and spoke about the matter. For its absolution, they summoned the occult practitioner Thrivikraman Bhatt from the outskirts of northern *Malabar*. His cult was oriented on a bloody pact he had made with the malevolent spirits and the darker forces. There was an arrogant monster in him who wanted to rule all elements. The story of the mother and the mystery girl reached Thrivikraman's ears too. The people of Chittezham offered him many rewards, including a significant portion of the land, if he could expel the ominous females.

The village grandiloquently celebrated his entry to Chittezham. On one full moon night at the end of summer, the six-foot-tall human beast stepped into the *Kavu*. With his arrival, Viruthiyar turned red. Nature stood droopy. Lives became dispirited.

Colourful patterns were laid at the edge of the grove and the lit-up *diyas* were kept in rows. Thrivikraman initiated invoking the dark forces. His commands rained with a malicious grin. He sent his attendants to fetch the five-year-old Kunjikkali. The protective mother had already taken off her amulet and tied it around the girl's neck. She was adamant to stay by Kunjikkali.

The girl stood smiling at Thrivikraman. Flames danced in her eyes, but with something beyond comprehension. In the middle of *diyas*, she was glowing as an ethereal entity. To him, she was a vessel for the wicked spirits he would summon, a mere conduit for his evil acts.

There was another sinister plot to implement *Irikkappindam* (a peculiar custom in which a person is ritually declared dead while still alive, thereby facing complete eviction from a place). This plot targeted Kunjikkavu. Thrivikraman's aide made a woman's clay maquette on the ground, in front of the house. It was a symbolic representation of Kunjikkavu herself, to which they called forth her physical and spiritual essence to settle down. After many incantations, they made her husband Chandran Nair do the death rites in her name.

Inside the *Kavu*, the poor mother stood as a shield for her daughter. She became uncontrollably violent as the folk tried to drive her away by calling her '*Korothu Yakshi*.' She kept yelling at their scornful remarks and struggled to get back to her daughter until some men from the family and some of Thrivikraman's assistants grabbed her by her hair. Her pleas fell on deaf ears.

The callous men showed no mercy, and they brutally trampled and tossed her into the thickets, bruising her. They even dared to rip off the woman and dragged her further beyond the borders of Chittezham with a loud utterance, *'You are dead. Go to hell!'* The atmosphere swelled with their contemptuous waves of laughter. Kunjikkavu was devastated and groped for her *mundu* (a piece of clothing to cover the lower body) in the dark. She cried in excruciating pain, calling out for *Kali,* her godmother!

While at the *Kavu*, Kunjikkali was no longer a child. The fire burned fiercely in her eyes, consuming the innocence that resided within her. The cute little form gradually transformed into a force of raw power and unyielding wrath, embodying the confluence of all oddities, a manifestation of the enigmatic goddess *Kali* herself, emerging to aid and support the helpless woman. A single stare of hers could propel the assailants into the air. Many felt strangled by her mighty, dark arms that had bangles worn. Her messy tresses locked them in hold until they lost their final breath. Those hands that tried to malign and hunt down Kunjikkavu, those tongues that spat poison at Kunjikkavu, could never rise again after that night.

The villagers, gripped by fear, could hardly bear witness to the sight unfurled before them that fateful night. The might and prowess of the fiercest figure were beyond measure, leaving everyone awestruck and trembling in her presence. People scattered running around for their lives.

Thrivikraman stood frozen, as his grandiose plans began crumbling before him. He had envisioned her as a mere pawn in his dark cult and had anticipated the ability to subdue the power within her. But as he beheld the girl's transformation, he was gripped by a dreadful revelation - she was nothing like the evil spirits he had encountered before. Her power eclipsed their dark essence, turning every attempt futile.

The poor woman lay battered amidst the foliage. Kunjikkali's radiance illuminated the darkness of the thicket, casting a divine shield around her wounded form. It had been rumoured that the girl, in her benevolence, whisked away the bereaved woman to otherworldly plains. According to the lore, they had vanished by the grove, at the riverside.

It had been whispered and believed that the curse originated from the otherworldly beings themselves, casting a dark shadow over the existence of men at Chittezham. In this cursed land, boys rarely came into the world, and males in the lineage found no prosperity or abundance, their efforts perpetually thwarted by unseen forces. Even the cattle, symbols of wealth and sustenance, withered and struggled to thrive in the spectral soil.

Thrivikraman and other men, including Chandran Nair, couldn't breathe a sigh of relief after that. One by one, they coughed up blood and after much torment, eventually met their doom. As time went by, Viruthiyaru altered its course leaving an inlet by the grove. It was the same portion of the river where Kunjikkali retreated with her mother. Through the years, it remained a pond, a living monument!

After the awe-inspiring event, the area between the serpent grove and the pond became known as *Kalikavu.* The name was a fitting reminder of the mother and the daughter. Locals also referred to it as *Kalikulam*. (*'Kulam'* means pond in Malayalam.) The night was forever etched in people's memories, a haunting testament to the girl's indomitable spirit and a woman's resilience.

Over time, the village realised the gravity and depth of the curse that had plagued the land. Some saw the girl as a direct manifestation of the fearsome goddess *Kali* herself. Others, more fearful and uncertain, thought she was a ghostly presence that had crossed over the realm of spirits, invited through the secret, unexplainable powers of Kunjikkavu.

Some even believe that Thrivikraman's wizardry unleashed darker spirits that night. Regardless of their specific interpretations, all agreed that the land had a tearful story of an innocent woman's endurance, faith, wrath, and vengeance.

The essence of haunting chants lingered in the howling winds, and sorrow manifested in the cries of the afflicted. It's said that on new moon nights, *Kalikavu* giggled and wept like children and women. At the seventh hour after sunset, a lantern could be seen moving by the pond's edge. The grove and the river remained silent repositories of ancient secrets. Viruthiyaru's perennial ripples still whisper this lore.

❖ ❖ ❖

Hundreds of infants were struggling to get out of the grave. Their cries overlapped each other and were heard as if from some nearby terrain. Cries of the stillborn.

Charulatha jolted awake and frantically covered her ears. The clock had struck four. She knew that it was neither a part of an early morning dream nor a figment of imagination, but a haunting reality that had plagued a land for generations. The story had been deeply embedded in her since she was a small girl. *Kalikavu* of Chittezham often beckoned her.

The fan spun at full speed. The clipped pages she was writing flapped continuously calling back her attention. She continued...

❖ ❖ ❖

CHAPTER 3

PARVATHY

The darkest hour of the night was still and weird. The woman's agonising wails filled the air, echoing in the dimly lit room. The midwife Janu's eyes flickered with the mixture of concern and despair, for this child, too, was different. Her hands were trembling as she took it out.

"*Ente Bhagavathi... para daivangale...*" (Oh my goddess, divine deities of the house...)

The *pooja* room was thronged with Amminiyamma's long sighs. Her ringed eyes were like two dry wells aimlessly cast at the dark corners of the place. Everyone realised it was a boy, for it emerged into the world without a voice, condemned to silence from the very first moment. Parvathy, pale and tormented by yet another tragic loss, delivered her third child to the grasp of death, just as she had with her previous babies. The weight of sorrow consumed her, rendering her silent for countless days. A mother with no children! The family could not find solace in the wake of such heartrending circumstances.

The curse manifested on its own, weighing down primarily the women at Chittezham. From a certain point in time, adherence to matriarchy became a common feature of *Nair* families. Women were the chief caretakers in the family. Time had silently witnessed all the disasters and bits of joy at Chittezham.

Parvathy of Cholayil House came there as the bride of Ramanunni, the only son of Chittezham Amminiyamma. Amminiyamma had been blind since childhood. The poor woman became a widow when she was pregnant at a very young age.

Ramanunni was her sole beacon of hope. Despite his many health struggles, he had endured the crippling effects of polio, which left him paralysed before he even turned five. In the face of these challenges, and the ominous curse hanging over her family's legacy, Amminiyamma raised him with unwavering determination.

Whispers of the curse circulated among those who knew the tale, and many doubted how Amminiyamma could ever have a male heir. She lived in constant turmoil, tormented by the weight of her fears, and fought tirelessly to shield her son from all harm. Yet, despite her relentless efforts, Ramanunni grew into a fragile and indecisive man, his nature shaped by the very insecurities he had been born into.

It was on a fateful day in the dry April that Parvathy first met Ramanunni. At that time, she was attending class at a weaving institute south of *Koodalmanikyam temple*. The temple tusker Kavalappara Komban, ran amok, causing chaos and leading to a stampede.

The tusker was already notorious for its mischief and unruly nature. Parvathy found herself trapped inside the institute for what felt like an eternity, forced to witness the terrifying chaos unfold. The chief mahouts struggled in vain, unable to restrain the wild beast, while the others dared not come any closer, fearful of its unpredictable fury.

In the arid expanse of the dry paddy field, a daring *Pandara* (a Hindu caste) teenager claimed to possess the knowledge of *Marma therapy* and the secret to taming wild elephants. Against the backdrop stood the restless tusker, its colossal form casting a surreal presence.

Fear and anticipation hung heavy in the air as the boy approached the tusker unarmed. Mustering courage, he seized a stone, and with a swift and unerring throw, the stone struck right in the middle of the Komban's forehead. For a few seconds, the frantic tusker transformed into a composed form. It remained with a penetrating gaze upon the youth. But that didn't stay long. A surge of primal rage burst within the beast, breaking it into an uncontrollable frenzy. It aimed at its tormentor.

It was a heart-pounding chase. As the teenager fought for life, evading the wrathful charge of the tusker, he stumbled across one of the dykes and collapsed to the ground. In a desperate bid for survival, he feigned death. The tusker slowly slinked away, keeping an eye cunningly on the fallen. The boy raised his head slightly to ensure the monster's retrieval when his eyes locked with those of the same.

The momentary respite suddenly altered to a cruel twist of fate. The boy's fate had been sealed in the unforgiving gaze of the tusker. Having smelled deception, it turned to the boy with seething anger. Its thundering footsteps shook the very earth beneath them. With a relentless thirst for revenge, the tusker lunged at the boy. It was determined to trample him underfoot. The tusks flung him into the air. The boy was mercilessly thrown to the fringes. His body lay motionless in a pool of crimson.

Like a dark conqueror of the woods claiming its territory, trumpeting its triumph, Komban retreated to the nearby temple pond for a sumptuous bath. It was a usual act for the tusker Kavalappara Komban to take immersion in temple ponds after each of his gory conquests.

Parvathy was the only one who had to stay inside the institute while the gruesome scene unfolded outside the field. Ramanunni was a visitor to the temple premises and happened to be there amidst the folks. While struggling to escape the stampede, he reached the building, panting, where Parvathy was hiding. She was greatly relieved to find a human presence near and signaled him to take the hideout.

At one moment, the tusker even advanced towards the small building. But fate intervened, and Parvathy's fortune took an unexpected turn as the attention of the enraged Komban was swiftly diverted by the arrival of the *Pandara* boy.

Both stood aghast, witnessing the spine-chilling incident, and Ramanunni, with his senses overwhelmed, passed out. A wave of panic washed over Parvathy and she rushed to his side to aid him. A spark of affection gleamed in their eyes, kindling an undeniable attraction between them. Her compassion, presence of mind, and timely support took Ramanunni's breath away.

Though in love, Ramanunni was reluctant to consider marriage. He didn't want to bring the girl into his dismal life. His obsession with the notion that he was an insignificant being and the lingering presence of the curse overshadowed everything.

But as days went by, an irresistible yearning grew in Ramanunni, creating a formidable dilemma. He detailed everything to his mother, which made Amminiyamma much more anxious about him.

"Unni, shall we call the broker to assist?".

Ramanunni didn't say a word to his mother. She called the astrologer Damodara Panicker to read Ramanunni's horoscope to see if his time favoured marriage. Panicker knew the family well. His simple 'yes' was a source of great relief to Amminiyamma.

Parvathy's parents had passed away when she was small. Her childhood was spent in dire poverty. She was brought up under so many restrictions in terms of the pride that was so much woven into the traditional domestic structure. Her brother Krishnan Nair was harsher to her, mostly.

Parvathy's wish to join the job as a needlework tutor in a private institute incurred the displeasure of Krishnan Nair's mistress.

"A girl going to work! What if she defames our family's good name!"

The lady whispered to Krishnan Nair in a tone of wonder and sorrow. This added to the disapproval already expressed by Parvathy's brother and relatives. They considered it beneath their family's prestige to have a woman working outside the confines of their home. Parvathy's defiance of her decision further aggravated the tension within the household, and she finally had to quit.

Krishnan Nair was initially unwilling to marry her off to Chittezham. In those days, it was common for married couples to have a significant age gap. But Krishnan Nair attempted to dissuade her by highlighting their age difference of around fifteen years. However, her love for Ramanunni was too strong for him to refute. Eventually, Krishnan Nair relented. Parvathy's relatives were taken aback by the news of her decision to marry into the Chittezham family. The entire village shared the same sentiment.

Like all brides, Parvathy had woven vivid, colourful dreams about the moments she would share with her husband. She envisioned their first night together, filled with joy and tenderness, blissfully ignorant of the storm that awaited her. She had been naive in her delight, certain that the man she loved would sweep her into a world of warmth and affection. But what awaited her was nothing like she had imagined—nothing short of a bewildering nightmare.

The night of their wedding spiralled into chaos when, as though overtaken by some unseen force, Ramanunni suddenly bolted from his room, completely naked, his body trembling with frantic, delirious energy. Parvathy stood frozen in horror, her mind struggling to comprehend the madness unfolding before her eyes. The man she had once dreamed of being with was now a stranger, lost in a fevered frenzy.

As if that wasn't enough, Parvathy was greeted by Amminiyamma's melancholic wails upon her arrival at the house. The older woman's sorrowful laments and gloomy predictions only deepened the sense of dread that had already settled in Parvathy's mind.

Amminiyamma had warned her, her voice heavy with caution, not to set foot inside *Kalikavu*. Yet, despite the warnings, Parvathy couldn't ignore the pull of something deeper, something beyond fear. It was a quiet, irresistible call of sympathy that led her towards the place. Instead of recoiling in terror, Parvathy found herself uncannily drawn to *Kalikavu*, feeling a divine, inexplicable connection to it as though her soul had always belonged there.

Parvathy was the pillar that held Ramanunni together. She was his tower of strength, a steady presence in his turbulent life. Yet, her own struggles were endless. Ramanunni's small business ventures constantly faltered, unable to withstand his naivety and poor decisions. Each failure piled onto the next, dragging them deeper into misery.

The weight of her losses crushed Parvathy's spirit. After losing three babies in consecutive pregnancies, she was left a shell of herself, emotionally and physically battered by the pain of each heartbreak. The stillborn children were laid to rest in the southwest of the land, and there, amidst her grief, she planted a breadfruit sapling—a fragile hope growing from the ashes of despair. She spent countless hours by it, pouring all her love and care into it, as if nurturing it could somehow heal the wounds in her soul.

Things were not easy for Ramanunni either. He became more fragile than ever, intimidated by a deep fear of snakes and darkness that only seemed to worsen his condition. His peers started teasing him whenever they saw him, calling out to him 'snake', to get a laugh out of it.

It had been a time that tested Parvathy's resilience, despite the immense pain she had endured. In all circumstances, she sought solace in her faith and navigated her arduous journey of healing and finding strength.

Seeing how nature can bring peace to our souls is always refreshing. Parvathy gradually began getting exposed to the forbidden corners of *Kalikavu* against Amminiyamma's edicts. She was like a symbiote, in perfect communion with the surroundings, which relieved her.

While Amminiyamma grumbled about situations, Parvathy contemplated, confessed, and introspected. Rituals and poojas that had been dormant for ages were reignited with Parvathy's arrival. She infused the grove with a renewed sense of faith and devotion, and the atmosphere became resonant with intense prayers.

The age was indeed one that had been facing extreme poverty, famine, and unemployment after World War I. Its ghostly hold disseminated a heavy burden on lives. Things were relatively stagnant, marred by some maladies or the other. Parvathy struggled hard to meet both ends as the only stable member at Chittezham. She was an ardent follower of Gandhiji and was much attracted to his idea of boycotting foreign clothes.

Like many others across the nation at the time, Parvathy wanted to promote indigenous clothing in the wake of Gandhi's decision to change his attire. Her decision had already been thwarted before marriage, and things did not change after marriage either. Though she was a meticulous weaver, her passionate efforts were hampered, and she couldn't take part in the mission due to her domestic circumstances.

Life went on. Ramanunni's delusions kept sparking tension. Meanwhile, Parvathy's faith remained stronger and after the three losses, she embraced motherhood.

❖ ❖ ❖

CHAPTER 4

WHERE SHADOWS FALL

"Ammaa... Unni..."

The desperate screams of the twelve-year-old girl broke through the tumultuous downpour. Parvathy couldn't hear what Rajam said. Her vision was blurred in the heavy rain. It had been pelting continuously for two weeks. Viruthiyaru overflowed with its terrible beauty, ravaging everything in its path. Its turbulent waters took multiple courses to wreak havoc around.

"Unni poyi... " (Unni is lost.)

Rajam cried out in anguish.

"Where is he, Ammu?"

Tears flowed from the mother, blending with the rain. When the tragedy struck, they were crossing the *Peruvallippadam* (field *Peruvalli*), burdened with provisions. Parvathy's toddler son, Unnikrishnan, was in the arms of her eldest daughter, Rajalakshmi. The child slipped from her hands and fell into the dyke's drainage that linked to the canal.

The distraught mother plunged into the water and fumbled her way towards where her son had drowned. Pieces of logs were wedged in the opening to the canal from where her lanky arms pulled up the little one. The child was wriggling in suffocation. She pressed his tummy against her chest. He spewed a few times and then started crying.

"My Unni..."

Parvathy smiled at him, tears of joy streaming down her face. Amidst the chaos, she lost the sack of dehusked rice she had collected from Koloor *Mana* (*Mana* is the residence of *Namboothiris*).

It was the Malayalam year 1116 (July 1941) when the torrential rain engulfed all the farmlands, destroying each crop and leaving the people on the brink of starvation. Parvathy had witnessed another appalling face of a flood, seventeen years back, from then (the flood of Malayalam year 1099, 1924 July), which had wiped off everything from *Parasuram's* soil. (The state of Kerala is believed to have been created by the *Sage Parasuram*.)

Strokes of destitution and years of unrelenting stress transformed Parvathy's physical appearance. Once a plump youth, she became utterly emaciated. After Rajalakshmi (Rajam or Ammu), she gave birth to their second daughter, Kochammu (Kochu), and then their son, Unnikrishnan (Unni). Amminiyamma had been bedridden for quite some time by then.

The arrival of the two girls filled their home with joy and brought a new ray of sunshine into their lives. Ramanunni's tea shop, located opposite the Viruthi temple road, thrived day by day. During this period, his friend Rappai offered him an opportunity to move to Ceylon to help run a hotel business. Parvathy was pregnant with Unnikrishnan when Ramanunni left. Over three years, she received only two letters from him.

Krishnan Nair's visits to Chittezham were mostly a blessing to Parvathy, as people seldom visited the house. After his wife's demise, he had been living alone without an heir. His frequent support came almost to an end with his second marriage.

With her children and an ailing mother-in-law home, Parvathy lived a meagre life, struggling hard to balance everything alone. They mostly survived on seasonal fruits like mangoes and jackfruits, showing gratitude for each harvest nearby. She wove clothes and did bits of cultivation.

Parvathy seamed breast clothes for women at Koloor *Mana*. All women, especially the youngest one, Subhadra of *Mana*, preferred Parvathy to prepare their garments. In the beginning, Parvathy was timid about visiting such upper-caste residences.

"Parutty, no worries, you can wear a *raukka* (blouse). Don't stop visiting me." Subhadra lovingly called Parukkutty as Parutty.

Subhadra's words instilled confidence in Parvathy. Those days, only the most upper-caste women and sometimes *Nair* women also had reservations about covering their breasts.

Parvathy would spend hours at Koloor. Subhadra was twenty years younger than Parvathy. The girl possessed a prismatic charm, like morning dew glistening on a lush leaf. Her large, deep brown eyes were reminiscent of a doe's, usually sans kohl. The svelte girl always wore an elegantly tapered emerald pendant that highlighted her golden glow. Subhadra's thin lips were never weary of smiling at those around her. Her cheeks were beautifully punctuated with dimples enhancing a youthful innocence. When she spoke and laughed, her voice was husky and melodious, harmonizing with the soft jingle of her silver anklets. With each stride, her long curly hair danced playfully, bouncing rhythmically behind her.

Subhadra's guidance helped Parvathy develop a keen interest in Sanskrit and *slokas*. Parvathy made her hair and taught her needlework. They enjoyed being together and learning the steps of *Thiruvathirakkali* (one traditional group dance form of Malayali women). They discussed situations, art, festivals, education, women, nation, injustices, and almost everything privately. Sometimes they dreamed of independence.

"When will we be independent, Parutty?"

Subhadra would fire an unexpected question to which Parutty would assert with pride.

"Didn't you still hear about Gandhi? He will settle everything. You know, he is going to get us freedom."

Subhadra would nod with a blank stare.

"Not that Parutty. Men are here also, fighting for the same cause. But when will we be free? Why didn't you get your education at the facility near the temple?"

Subhadra would then sigh, hurling an aimless gaze to the distance, and then would ask.

"Was Kunjikkavu free? The Whites were not here then, right?"

Most of their conversations would end up in some rhetoric, perplexing Parvathy.

"I don't know, Subhadrakkutty; that confuses me."

Parvathy would pass a slit of smile artificially. But those words made her thoughtful, leaving her heart heavy with the image of Kunjikkavu.

Subhadra was like a godsend, and she always assured Parvathy of timely help. They became close after Parvathy lost her babies.

"Parutty, I know what it means to a mother to lose her children. It is even much more painful for a child to thrive in the absence of its mother. I haven't seen my mother.

My father's other consorts cannot make it. Nothing good happens to me. I wish my mother were with me now. She would have erased all my woes and worries!" She paused for a while and continued, "Will you do that for me?"

Parvathy would sob then, knowing not to console Subhadra and herself. She would hold some salt, mustard seeds, and dry chillies tight in her palm, never letting them see the skies, and then bring them in front of Subhadra, moving them around her face three times. She would eventually let them temper in the traditional hearth.

"Subhadrakkutty will never get evil eyes. You will reign as a princess."

Subhadra's eyes would bloom with affection and gratitude towards Parutty. She believed Parvathy had the protective power to avoid all misfortunes.

"Well, I will not have children. I cannot marry. You know, my horoscope has *chovva dosham*." (Astrological finding in one's horoscope, as per the planet Mars' influence on the person)

Subhadra would laugh hilariously calling...

"Krishnaa..."

Subhadra's joy knew no bounds when she heard that Parvathy had given birth to Unnikrishnan. Though she wanted to see the baby, she had no permission to leave her *Mana*.

After Unni turned one, Parvathy brought her children to Koloor. Subhadra hugged Parutty. Her eyes were wet as she kissed Unni. She sewed clothes, dressed him up, and uttered with a peal of laughter.

"What else do you want, Parutty? You have Krishnan everywhere! Do one thing. Let Unnikrishnan be mine; you have your brother Krishnan..."

Parutty was silent for a second and burst into tears.

"Oh, dear. Nothing will happen to Unni. You can protect him from all evil eyes as you do to me. You are his mother."

Subhadra took Unni to the cowshed to show him the adorable newborn calf and its mom. The baby was bunting its mother's udder. Subhadra pampered Unni, laughing heartily at the calf's cute movements.

"Hey Unni, do you want this baby?" She asked in a mirthful tone.

"*Oppa* (The word *Oppa* is addressed to an elder brother, by sister, especially in some castes.) once brought a cow with its calf there. It was after Ammu's (Rajam's) birth. He thought a milking cow would grace the house and would be good to nourish me as a feeding mom. But..."

Parutty spoke with downcast eyes, recalling Nandini and Meenu. The incident replayed in her mind once again, afresh.

***

"Krishnaa ", Amminiyamma said, "Take them back to your place, dear. Why should we bring suffering to these poor creatures?"

Krishnan Nair ignored her words. Amminiyamma was determined to keep the cow away from the grove. Parutty took great care of the mother cow and the calf, following her mother-in-law's advice. She named them Nandini and Meenu. Those were days of joy. Meenu grew with her mischievousness.

One day, Meenu was tied in the eastern corner of the land, while Nandini was in the barn. It was noon, and Parutty was looking for plantain leaves. Suddenly, she heard strange lowings coming from the barn. Upon reaching the spot, she saw Nandini gazing toward the west. In her search, Parutty couldn't find Meenu where she had been tied. She rushed to where Nandini was focused and found Meenu stuck beneath the bushes. Her rope had accidentally come loose and got caught in the thickets. The poor thing staggered along the slippery ground, desperately struggling to breathe.

Parvathy had no one nearby to call for help. Ramanunni had already left for the Guruvayur temple the previous day. Not knowing what else to do, Parutty threw the knife in her hand towards the rope, hoping it would cut it and free the cow. But it was too late to save her.

Kattuparambil Ityara, the butcher who lived behind the church grounds, came running to claim the carcass. Meenu was just money to him, effortlessly obtained. Parutty was hesitant to accept the money he offered. Her pain doubled when she saw Nandini wailing inside the barn.

"Somebody has to take her off from here. Let him take, daughter."

Amminiyamma mumbled to Parutty.

"Ityara, don't let the mother cow see any of this."

There was a forced strength in Amminiyamma's voice. Parutty could feel the depth of her distress.

Ityara cleared everything as requested. That day, Parutty didn't feel like feeding Ammu. Nandini was all alone in her shed. She neither chewed the cud nor drank anything. Parutty could sense what it meant for Nandini.

She sent for her brother and pleaded with him to take Nandini back. By then, she fully realised the weight of Amminiyamma's judgements.

"At least she can be saved, *Oppe* (in a tone of calling). I cannot bear to see her in tears."

"You silly girl, animals don't cry."

"She is right. They do, son. Mothers do too."

There was no emotion in Amminiyamma's words.

❖ ❖ ❖

"Did he take Nandini?"

Subhadrakkutty, who was deeply moved by Parutty's description, asked, and Parutty nodded in response.

Subhadra hosted Parvathy's children and made them eat to their fill. The generous girl always managed to save money and gave whatever she had, to her close ones.

Parvathy gifted Subhadra with a hand-loomed red blouse on *Onam*. Subhadrakkutty looked uniquely beautiful in it.

A few months later, Subhadra disclosed a secret to Parvathy, that she was in love with a *Nair* boy named Chandu. In those days, she used to ask Parvathy how she had met Ramanunni. However, things got worse as her father and uncles caught her affair. Subhadra was facing a grave situation. For the first time, she raised a question to her male relatives.

"Why do you people have a relationship with *Nair* women? Why can't I choose a man from the same?"

After that, Subhadra didn't see daylight for many days. She was kept inside a ventless room by the side of the granary. Parvathy couldn't meet her, though she tried to converse with her from outside.

"Parutty, save me from here."

Subhadra's words saddened Parutty. Her absence choked Parvathy inside. There was no way to help out the poor girl. Every gleeful moment they had, came to a pause.

Anger frothed within the *Mana* inmates, and finally, they found Sankaranarayanan, an affluent, middle-aged man with high prospects for the future, as Subhadra's groom-to-be. Their horoscopes matched, too.

Subhadra was forced to marry him and after that, she was never the same as before. She rarely visited Koloor. Parutty met her twice there after that. The girl became rather reticent. A new bride's jollity was lacking in her. Parvathy noticed some red marks of lashing behind Subhadra's neck once.

"What's that? Tell me. Did he hurt you?"

Subhadra didn't speak a word. She remained pale with her usual stare. That day, as Parvathy was leaving Koloor, Subhadra approached her with a smile. She wore the same red blouse, which Parutty had gifted. For a long time, they remained silent, and Subhadrakkutty eventually broke it. Her voice was feeble as she said it,

"I can take birth, ten times, as a dog. But I no longer want to be born as a Namboothiri woman.

"What's happening to you Subhadrakkutty? Tell me..."

"I will be back to you, Parutty."

That was the last time they met. After that Parvathy went to Koloor many times, with the hope to meet the girl.

"Won't Subhadrakkutty come for *Vishu*?" (*Vishu* is a festival marking the beginning of an astronomical year.)

Parvathy would enquire.

"Not sure this time." Subhadra's aunt put it bluntly.

Parvathy couldn't frequent Koloor after Amminiyamma got bedridden.

Once rain ruined everything, Parvathy got stuck at home for days and all provisions ran out. She would walk to the granary with a vain hope of getting a handful of rice. The hearth remained cold with proliferated moulds. An overwhelming need for things compelled Parvathy to seek some assistance from *Mana*.

❖ ❖ ❖

Parvathy kissed Unni. Subhadra's words uncannily echoed within her,

'... Nothing will happen to Unni. You can protect him from all evil eyes as you do to me. You are his mother.'

Parvathy took off her *veshti* (A long piece of clothing that is used to cover the upper body.) and tied it around Unni, keeping him close to her body.

'The rice!' She thought. The sack was missing. With her son, she waded through the water, tightly holding onto Rajam. As she moved, she searched for the lost sack underwater. Looking up at the sky, she let out a loud utterance of relief, *"ente Viruthiyattinkkarayappaa..."* (Calling the deity of the Viruthi temple, here *Lord Shiva*) and then summoned all her might to heave and pull up the damp, heavy sack home.

Viruthiyaru submerged a significant portion of the village during a single night. The surroundings of Chittezham grew darker and denser with heavy cloud bursts. Parvathy panicked, realising the severity of the situation. The heavy downpour drowned out her cries for help. By then, Unni had developed a high temperature.

After settling the younger ones inside the *machchu* (Malayalam word for attic—here, it's the typical traditional attic.), Parvathy and Rajam struggled to climb up, carrying Amminiyamma. She had already stashed the rice up there. The place couldn't hold a person at full length, so Parvathy had to hunch herself through the attic. She also took the cat Ponnu up there.

Before the nightfall, she had prepared rice gruel and fed them all. Amminiyamma was trembling under the blanket. Parvathy sat by her, holding her children closer.

"Amma, will the water come here too?"

Rajam's question shook Parvathy. In the dim light of the lantern, Parvathy saw the frightened faces of her little ones, drenched more in tears than in water.

"No, my darlings. This will stop. Don't be afraid. I am here with you."

Parvathy made them repeat after her, chanting synonyms of *Arjuna* (the third one among the *Pandava brothers* in the *Epic Mahabharata*) to keep them from fear.

Arjunan Phalgunan Parthan Vijayanum

Vishruthamaya per pinne kireediyum

Shwethavahanan Dhananjayan Jishnuvum

Bheethiharam Savyasachi Bheeb*hatsuvum*

Pathu naamangalum bhakthyaa japikkilo

Nithya bhayangal akannupom nishchayam

(Arjuna, Phalguna, Partha, and Vijaya,

Then the famed name Kiriti,

Shwethavahana (one with white chariot), Dhananjaya (winner of wealth), and Jishnu (the conqueror),

Bheethihara (remover of fear), Savyasachi (ambidextrous archer), and Bheebhatsu (one who despises wrongdoing),

If one devoutly recites these ten names,

All constant fears will surely vanish.)

Amminiyamma's lips moved rhythmically as they chanted. The sound of their recital reverberated through the attic. As Parvathy breastfed Unni, she couldn't help but have numerous questions. She gently sponged the boy, now and then, with a wet cloth.

After putting the children to sleep, she searched and found a spot to remove the roof tile, just in case the water level rose further and they needed to escape the attic. A little mouse squeaked under Ponnu's paws. Parvathy lowered the lantern's flame and stayed awake, keeping a vigilant eye out. The rain kept pouring.

“Ammaa, water...” the children called out to her.

“ When did I even sleep!”

She wondered, her heart sinking as she caught sight of her children drowning. Her veins got numb. She dove into the water, desperately reaching out to them. But her kids were deep in the water, fighting for their lives. Suddenly, she felt those little arms. Those of Unni. But there was a whirlpool surrounding him. Parvathy screamed and fainted, leaving everything black.

“Parutty, wake up, save me from here. I can’t breathe...”

Anklets chimed somewhere. A familiar voice woke her up.

“Subhadrakkutty...is it you?”

Parvathy opened her eyes. The rain had already stopped. There was no water or whirlpool inside the attic. All were sleeping peacefully. It was all a dream.

‘Who was here?’ She mused.

The lantern’s faint glow flickered in the darkness. Parvathy rose and moved towards it, her eyes instinctively drawn to the scene outside. There, perched atop the wall, was the cat Ponnu, eyes fixed on the west, its gaze unblinking and intense. Something shifted along the edge of *Kalikavu*, caught in her peripheral vision. She peered through the narrow gaps between the wooden planks and the broken roof tiles, straining to identify the figure. It seemed as if someone was walking with a lantern, its light bobbing in the distance. But that couldn't be, not in that part of the land—the grove had been completely flooded, the waters rising far higher than any person could traverse.

A sudden, sharp spark of realisation jolted Parvathy to her core. Without hesitation, she ran towards Unni. She reached for him, her hands trembling as she checked for warmth. The little body was cold, unnaturally so. Panic surged through her veins, and in a wild frenzy, she shook him, her voice breaking as she called out his name, desperation lacing every syllable.

"Unni, you can't go. Devi... (goddess), give me my son back. It's not possible. Ammoppol and Kochoppol (*Oppol* means elder sister. Here, sisters Rajalakshmi and Kochammu) are here waiting for you. Achamma (father's mother) is calling you. Come back Unni..."

She pressed his pale lips against her nipple, hoping he would open his eyes again.

If time could speak, it would be through silence.

Her voice became weak. She sat down and raved indistinctly. The old woman in the bed was voiceless. Her tears were the only evidence that she was still alive.

Rajam and Kochammu stood stupefied in front of their mother. They spent a long time in the attic. Rajam continuously checked the water level, and before noon, her uncle Krishnan Nair arrived at Chittezham in a raft with some men. The scene that awaited them was heartbreaking.

"*Oppe*.." (Calling her brother)

Parvathy went on lamenting. The sight of her holding Unni and the intensity of her grief broke everyone's heart. The trauma left her irreversibly lost. It was even more challenging to separate the boy's body from Parvathy.

"*Oppe*, lay him under the breadfruit tree. His father hasn't even met him yet. I can show him when he returns. Let them all sleep together there."

Parvathy giggled.

Krishnan Nair kept silent and slowly took the boy away.

The next day, by evening, the water receded by a quarter. There was no trace of rain clouds either. Viruthi was a small village that absorbed the shock deep into its very being. The flood's impact was heavy, affecting the majority of areas in and around *Kochi* and *Valluvanadu kingdoms*.

Parvathy and the others were shifted to a high ground on the outskirts of Viruthi. After a three-day stand there, they returned to Chittezham. Upon their return, Parvathy expressed her wish to see Subhadrakkutty. Krishnan Nair evaded her demand. He told her they wouldn't be able to because the fields were still wet. Whenever she mentioned Subhadra's name, he would divert to other topics. One week later, Krishnan Nair gave the news to Parvathy.

"Koloor Subhadra is no more." He added after a pause, "They say, she hanged herself. She was in Bombay, at her husband's."

There were no tears, no sighs from Parvathy. She leaned against the wall.

The last of his words shuddered her, bringing her the echo of someone lost.

"Same night of our Unni's departure."

❖ ❖ ❖

CHAPTER 5

AMMOPPOL AND THAMBRATTIYAMMA

It was the late 80s, and Madras Medical College Hospital stood proudly with its grand red-brick heritage. Walking through the corridors of the hospital building was a hefty woman in her fifties. She gracefully wore a well-pleated white sari and matching blouse. Her face radiated like a full moon with a big round red *bindi* on her forehead. She had dyed hair neatly secured in a bun with a thin, almost invisible hairnet, adorned with a few U-pins. As she entered the seminar hall, the clock chimed eight, and her pleasant face suddenly turned to one of annoyance.

"Good morning, Ma'am," the cheerful greetings came in unison. However, the woman didn't seem too pleased to greet them back. For a moment, she glanced at the picture of Florence Nightingale hanging above the board. With a book on Practical and Nursing Management in her hand, she placed it down and adjusted her glasses before turning her attention to the board.

Three girls in nurses' uniforms came running to the entrance and politely asked, "Shall we come in, Madam?"

"No," the woman replied without showing her face. "You may go elsewhere and get some fresh air." Her words dripped with contempt. The girls pleaded with her further.

"I don't accept apologies." She said callously, dispersing the girls and commanding them to meet her later at the cabin. After a demanding two-hour session, she gathered the nurses for a briefing. Her tone remained professional but firm as she outlined the medical strategies they would be implementing.

"Make sure every patient is attended to. No one should be left alone, not for a second," she instructed, her voice brokering no room for excuses.

She paused for a moment, allowing the weight of her words to sink in.

"Negligence might be tolerated in some places, but not here," she continued, her eyes scanning the nurses as she spoke.

"You are expected to be vigilant, to give nothing less than your best. If you're unsure or need assistance, Sr. Tamilarasi will provide further guidance."

With that, she concluded the meeting with a swift nod. "That's all for today. Thank you."

Her gaze softened slightly, but only for a moment before she turned and left, her presence lingering in the room long after she'd departed.

After a meeting with the DMO, she commenced her general rounds at the hospital. Waiting outside her cabin, where the nameplate read *C. Rajalakshmi, Assistant Director of Medical Services (Nursing),* were the girls. Sr. Rajalakshmi entered her cabin and permitted the girls to come in.

"Madam, we were late for class. It was only fifty seconds, and we apologise for that," explained the students.

"This isn't the first time you've been late. This profession requires punctuality above all else. I need a written explanation. Being late is not acceptable in the medical field. Now, all of you can leave."

Rajalakshmi interrupted one of the students who tried to explain their side, including health issues.

"You, stop. I know who is telling the truth and who isn't. Now, all of you can leave," Rajalakshmi stated firmly.

It was 12:45 pm, and Rajalakshmi was about to leave for her apartment when the attendee brought her a bunch of letters.

"It's lunchtime. You could have brought it a bit earlier," Rajalakshmi remarked.

The attendee scratched his head and left. Rajalakshmi randomly placed the letters on her desk, and as she did, she accidentally came across a postcard which read :

Dear Ammoppol,

How are you Oppol? It has been a year since Amma left us. Unni is leaving for Kashi tomorrow. As you know, he wants to immerse half of her ashes there. He got a promotion and was transferred to Thiruvananthapuram. He joined there last week. He has sent you a letter. Didn't you get it? Our girl is not okay without Amma and Kodi here. We are coming there. We will start from here after Vishu, on April 15th. Oppol, don't forget to do Amma's first annual rites on the 10th. See you soon.

Viruthi, Yours lovingly,

02/04/1989 Kochu

'Amma, I miss your casual notes here.' Rajalakshmi let out a sigh. She took a few letters and left for her apartment, weighed down by a terrible void.

❖ ❖ ❖

The night was calm. Madras was sweating buckets in the April heat. In the distance, the faint, rhythmic roars of the waves from Marina Beach reached Rajalakshmi's ears, a distant reminder of the world outside. She lay on her couch, clutching the letter tightly to her chest as if its weight might anchor her to the present. Her fingers trembled slightly as memories surged through her mind, uninvited but relentless. The letter, once a symbol of hope, now felt like a tether to the past, pulling her deeper into a sea of thoughts she had tried to bury.

It was solely Rajam's decision to accept her uncle's suggestion to join the nursing course at Coimbatore. The family had endured the harshest blows of destiny. Parutty bore the backlash of all hardships, particularly the one that unfolded inside the attic. The mystery clung to her like an unforgettable nightmare, and the image of Subhadrakkutty with her giggles frequently startled her from sleep. The words she had heard that night haunted her:

"Parutty, wake up, save me from here. I can't breathe..."

Parvathy firmly believed that Subhadrakkutty would never resort to suicide.

Amminiyamma passed away a few months after Unni's death. The poor woman had wanted to say something to Parutty before she left. A low wail escaped her as she called out for 'Ramu' (calling for Ramanunni, her son), and Parvathy noticed a turbulent darkness within the blind woman's eyes.

She exhibited restlessness and spoke incoherently throughout the entire day. As Parutty offered her water, she tenderly touched her and smiled, clasping her palms together. An expression, finally sought by her, of gratitude. Even as she passed away, her eyes remained open. Thus, a life spent in blindness, dedicated to praying for the well-being of her loved ones, came to an end.

Time stripped away its leaves.

Parvathy eagerly anticipated Ramanunni's return. As time passed, hope faded away, and he never came back. Eventually, Krishnan Nair took Parvathy and her children to Cholayil, offering them shelter. At first, people were sympathetic to her situation, but as time passed, that sympathy waned, replaced by cold indifference and somber expressions. Sarasu, Krishnan Nair's wife, grew increasingly anxious about the possibility of losing her husband's attention and wealth to his poor sister and her children. She couldn't shake the thought that the Nair family had a clear preference for girls, a notion that gnawed at her. She started constantly nagging her husband, urging him to send Parutty back to Chittezham. She tried to convince him by pointing out that it was solely Parvathy's decision to marry Ramanunni, and she must face the consequences of her choices.

She went on...

"Don't you see what's happening to people there? Why should we invite trouble into our lives? Let's forget about Parukkutty. Think about those girls. And don't forget the fact that they are Ramanunni's blood. If you want to give something to your sister, give it and send it. But never let them in here."

The thought hatched inside his mind, gradually making him worried. They were afraid that the shadows of Chittezham might creep into their house too. But even before he said anything, Parutty had already made up her mind to leave for Chittezham.

"*Oppe*, I have to go back. Their father could show up any minute. Imagine how he'd feel if he didn't see me there."

She didn't say anything further. Rajam, on the other hand, was thrilled about moving to Chittezham. She couldn't stand her mother's ancestral home anymore. Her growing intolerance made her push her mother to go back. A series of tough experiences made her mature beyond her years. She became the rock that her mother leaned on.

Both Rajam and Kochu never experienced their father's affection. Most of their childhood was spent amidst the shadows of the past and how they impacted their lives. Their problems were never acknowledged, and maybe they were never resolved either. They kept wavering in a constant cycle of hope and hopelessness.

Rajam was a living testament that shattered the common belief that children raised by single moms would be fragile. She was never one. The young lady lived by her own rules and convictions. Her personality exuded determination and resilience. Time witnessed that as well.

❖ ❖ ❖

Rajam made up her mind to become a nurse in 1947. It was an era that marked a time of joyous moments, and witnessed a nation's rising pride and rejuvenated hopes with its newly gained freedom from so many brunts. The soil had been waiting so long to celebrate, to accept, to change, to sustain after a plethora of challenges. Its repercussions were everywhere in the Indian subcontinent.

Against this background, Krishnan Nair took Rajam to Coimbatore to enroll in the nursing course. He was working as a driver there at that time. Parutty felt so worried about sending her daughter away to a far-off place. But in the end, she had to give in to Rajam's words.

"Amma, life isn't all about dwelling on hardships. Let's be practical. How long will we continue to sigh like this? Please, Amma, stop burdening yourself. I've decided to move on."

Rajam was a little over seventeen when she left for her studies. Things began to change when she pursued her vocation. For years, there used to be just non-sticky water in the rice gruel made by Parvathy. They never had a full meal to quell their hunger. Everything took a turn. The kitchen in Chittezham started getting the aroma of cooked rice.

Despite most people in the neighbourhood being afraid to enter Chittezham, Parutty never hesitated to help them during emergencies. She was always willing to forgo her meals to feed others in need, and because of this unselfishness, people came to adore her deeply.

In no time, she became a benevolent mother to all, with her gifted ability to cast out evils from people, especially children. Parents would bring their sick children to her to do away with the evil grip around them.

"*Thambrattiyamma*, (short form of *Thamburatti*, addressing a woman with respect, here with an added respect too for a mother), please see. There is something wrong with my child. He has a severe stomach ache."

Parutty would do something like all moms traditionally do. She would take salt, mustard seeds, and chilies, and then would perform the same procedure that she used to do for Subhadrakkutty.

The intensity of suffocation she felt after tempering the things in the fire decided the severity of the ailment. Afterward, the parents would seek some advice from her and leave.

There was another strange way in which she cured only children. The parent would be asked to bring a handful of rock salt in a jackfruit leaf, which she would hold in her hand, and then would go on talking to them continuously. In this method, the strength of the evil grip around the child would be gauged based on how many times she yawned during the conversation. If she got tired of too much yawning, parents took it as a bad sign and would do the needful care for the child afterward.

It was surprising for the people to see themselves and their children getting cured after Parutty's mysterious acts.

"Is there any sense in it, Amma?"

Parutty smiled at Rajam's question and then said.

"Ammu, it makes perfect sense. If you put your all senses into a single act, they won't fail you, my child."

Rajam couldn't make out.

"We all are mere fluids and senses," Parutty stated further.

❖ ❖ ❖

'Amma...', Rajalakshmi woke up from her couch, with her eyes wet.

In the distance, Marina was getting lulled by the waves into a serene sleep.

❖ ❖ ❖

CHAPTER 6

THE GIRLS IN THE MIRROR

I should remove the plastic from this photo. Years have passed since this picture was taken. The girl in it is me. The other face has faded so much. Still, she is so fresh in my memory. Those days are pristine to me, including the day when I made my maiden journey on a train. Train to Madras. Summers were not this hot then.

Memories dribbled out of Charulatha as she went on...

7:45 am, Madras Railway Station, 16 April 1989

Those streets of Madras (the present-day Chennai) were then nasty and smelled of human waste. Rajalakshmi despised the squalor and filth out there, but each speck of her heart was lost in the place, just as that of one lost in love. It was 8 am by her watch. She walked along the railways and waited on platform number three. She wore dark glasses, and her gaze shifted between her wrist and the eastward direction. The growing impatience was quite evident on her face.

The train rumbled into the tunnel, causing the girl to panic. That was least expected by her, sitting by the window seat and enjoying the reptilian beauty of the thing with which she had fallen in love at the first sight itself. It was, to her, like the series of soap covers stacked in a line by Kochoppol, in her almirah.

"You are going to get inside a snake, darling."

Kochoppol had already given her a clue. It was an alien exercise for her, though. Therefore, she couldn't take that bang. Her face complained of fear. *'Snakes in Viruthi never frightened me'*, she thought.

The train reached the station almost twenty-five minutes late. Kochammu got down from the train. She was a lean, gaunt woman with skin as pale as porcelain. The starkness of her complexion accentuated the delicate shadows of her angular features. Wisps of thinning hair clung desperately to her scalp, revealing the underlying contours of her head.

There was only embarrassment in the girl's eyes as she stood holding Kochoppol's hand. She skulked behind her *sari*, at the sight of Ammoppol. Rajalakshmi stared at the girl without any change in expression. She led them to the parking lot on the northern side. The girl's eyes widened with amazement as she got into a white Ambassador car.

She became curious and soon lost in sightseeing. The driver and Ammoppol went on talking about something. They spoke Tamil (the language spoken by the people of Tamil Nadu). The girl had heard the language spoken by Kodi and Ammoppol at Chittezham, and she could understand some of it only when spoken at a low pace. The car entered an avenue. The trees, mostly along the sides, were those of neem. In the new city, the tree was the only thing familiar to the girl. She had seen it in Viruthi too. She peeped at Ammoppol many times in an air of surprise. Rajalakshmi was sitting to the left of the driver. 'Such a Royal Queen!' The girl imagined being driven to a wonderland ruled by the queen, Ammoppol. *'One day, I will also sit in the front seat, like her.'* She thought.

They stopped in front of a four-storeyed building which appeared enormous to the girl. Their apartment was on the first floor, comprising one drawing room, lounge, kitchen, pantry, and a big bedroom with an attached bathroom.

There was an additional chamber, which was not open, adjacent to the bedroom. After breakfast, Rajalakshmi gave the girl a five-rupee coin as *Vishukkaineettam*. (The first monetary offering made by the older members to the younger ones, auspiciously during the season of *Vishu.*) She made them comfortable and told them that Lachu would bring their lunch. Soon, she left for the hospital.

A long array of windows could be seen on one side of the bedroom, which opened onto the neem trees in the front yard. An ornamental mirror was placed in the bedroom corner by those windows. It was oval and was shelved by ivory from both sides. She had never seen such a strange mirror until that day. *'Why have they kept elephant's tusks here?'* She wondered. Her attempts to reach the mirror were futile. Besides, there were no chairs for her to stand on.

Things that amused her were quite a few. The winding stairs, the grand sofa settee in the lounge, the European-style closet, the kitchen burner, and Ammoppol's cupboards, all in a colonial fashion, all attracted her greatly. Everything she tasted was different there.

By noon, there was a knock on the door. A girl, around twenty years old, appeared with the lunch carrier. She wore a yellow *davani*, (a simple outfit worn by young girls in South India) and her plaited hair was adorned with jasmine and crossandra.

"*Nan Adilakshmi. Madam enna Lachu nu koopduvanga. Avanga ungalukku madhiya sapadu anuppirukkanga*." (I am Adilakshmi. Madam calls me Lachu. She has sent lunch for you.)

She introduced herself with a smile in Tamil.

Kochoppol expected an elderly woman at the door.

Adilakshmi had all the charm of a typical Tamil girl. She had long hair and a lean physique. Her eyes always smiled more than her lips. She wore a nose pin, as generally worn by the Tamil women. She did the cooking and cleaning stuff in Rajalakshmi's apartment, and most of the days, she ate from there and would leave by evening.

"*Un peru enna*?" (What's your name?)

The girl was reluctant to respond to Adilakshmi.

"*Yen nee enkitte pesala*?" (Why are you not talking to me?)

She asked further. Kochoppol intervened, pointing out that the girl didn't know Tamil well, and she took Adilakshmi to the kitchen. Kochoppol spoke in a low voice. She came back from the kitchen, calling the girl,

"Latha... Can I call you so?" Lachu smiled at the girl who stood silent.

Lachu tried to get closer to her, and she promised that the city would hold so many sights and wonders for her. She cooked a variety of dishes for Latha. Sometimes, she fed her with her own hands. The girl had never seen chapatis made in Viruthi. It was Adilakshmi who introduced them along with her aromatic pea curry, which became her favourite. She called her *'Akka'* (addressing an older sister in Tamil). Lachu made the special, unique mirror in the bedroom, accessible to Latha with the help of a medium-height wooden stool. Latha looked in the mirror only when Lachu arrived; they mostly did it together.

Latha asked Lachu about the tusks.

"Are they original, Akka?"

"*Theriyallaye*" (I don't know.)

"What's original, what's duplicate? Who knows, dear!" Lachu's words expressed her ignorance.

With Kochoppol and Lachu, Latha visited places. Human excreta could be seen in some streets, and Latha had to hop like frogs to cross them. In the beginning, it was unbearable for her. But with time, she found it funny.

Lachu even took her to the inner areas, near her small residence, where people mostly lived by doing laundry services. Many natives were seen drying cow dung in masses. The girl expected the whole world would be like Viruthi, but it was not seen anywhere there. Viruthi was green like a parrot, and it smelled like sandalwood and jasmine dissolved in the night rain. But the new place stank. People there suffered the most from drought. Still, they smiled. They smiled at the girl also, as if they had known her for ages.

Lachu's father was bedridden. She could go to school only until grade four. After that, she had to abandon her studies for the sake of her family. Other members of her family had gone for their daily duties then. Lachu took the girl to a studio and took their photos. She taught her some letters in the Tamil alphabet too, and Latha promised she would learn all the letters in the future.

One day, Kochoppol was taken to the hospital due to an intense stomach ache. There, she underwent appendectomy at Ammoppol's hospital, and it was on her days of recovery that Latha developed symptoms of mumps. Lachu nursed her, fed her, and medicated her with proper care. She plucked the neem leaves, ground them, and applied them on the swelled-up areas around her chin and jaw. Parrots were the regular visitors in those neem trees. The girl's days broke mainly with the screeches of those birds.

"Are there seeds in those trees? Do the parrots eat them?"

Latha would ask.

"There are seeds, and they eat too."

Lachu's reply led to an argument and then to a peal of laughter.

"How come! Neem seeds are bitter. How do they eat them!? No way. Yuck!"

It was Lachu who cooked a variety of dishes on Latha's birthday. She even took her to the temple nearby. Within days, the girl found something peculiar and common familiar to the people she met in Madras. They always wanted to ensure that she had eaten something. Lachu Akka, some of the hospital staff who visited Ammoppol, the attender Murugesan, the pot-bellied man who brought a big box of ice cream for her, the auto driver Thangavel who took her with Lachu around, the photographer Arul, those three dark, fat women wearing nose rings on both sides, whom Ammoppol had called for clearing up lice from Latha's hair, and even that Doctor who vaccinated her on diagnosing mumps - all enquired about her wellness, by asking *'saptachaa?'* (Have you eaten something?). At one point, Latha even thought those people gave importance only to food! It took years for her to realise the value of those plain words and how important a simple gesture in life is.

4:15 pm, Marina Beach, Madras, 20 May 1989

The most memorable experience for Latha there was her visit to the first longest beach in India, Marina! That day, Ammoppol, Kochoppol, and Adilakshmi were with her. They arrived there after making it to M G R's memorial. An ever-lit lamp was there near the monument. Ammoppol spoke volumes about the portrait, there, of the man in dark glasses, in great pride, Dr. M G Ramachandran. Finally, she made it to Kochoppol,

"You know, Kochu, his father was a *Nair*," she said, her voice trailing off with the weight of the information.

The girl, growing weary of the long description and Kochoppol's constant 'yessing' in response, found herself distracted. As she studied the man's face, she couldn't help but notice its striking resemblance to Ammoppol's. Both wore dark glasses, and curiously, neither had a moustache.

Beyond them, the beach stretched out in all its beauty, the promenade enticing people from distant lands with its charm. Latha, holding Adilakshmi's hand, stood there, her impatience growing as she waited for the others to move forward.

There were too many people, including foreigners, strolling along the beach. Behind them was the beckoning waters of the Bay of Bengal, lying in a vast stretch. The girl stood agape. *'Kadal*!' ('the sea!') It had only been in her dreams. She had seen the pictures of it in her third-grade Malayalam textbook. She had heard that there was a sea almost fifteen kilometers away from her village, too. But no one had ever taken her to it. The force of her inner surge was so immense that it became one with that of the sea's magnificence. She couldn't help but walk faster towards its tidal line. It was as if she got drawn by something inexplicable. The girl's smile was complete as she moved.

Adilakshmi held her tightly, not letting her go further. But, after a while, they started playing together in the waves. She saw children making sand castles. Pigeons were pecking at the peanuts dropped by the visitors. People, including children, rode horses. The majority of those horses were white. She saw the creature for the first time and confirmed that it didn't have horns like the ones she had heard about in her Achamma's stories.

The sight of the semi-nude white men and women who lay and walked there roused laughter and wonder in the girl. Adilakshmi and Latha looked at each other, feeling somewhat intimidated by the presence of those people. They deliberately avoided staring at them. Latha's chuckles made Lachu laugh continuously.

"Lachu Akka, why are they lying like that?" Latha asked with a curious look.

"It's because there is no sun in their places."

Latha was surprised at the answer.

"*Ayyo*, that's impossible. Sun is everywhere!"

With the next remark made by Latha, both burst into laughter.

"They are like those *sambar chilies* (*Sambar* is a South Indian dish) dipped in buttermilk that Achamma and Kochoppol used to sundry at Chittezham."

After a few seconds, Lachu asked,

"Achamma is Madam's mother, right?"

"Not only her, but she is also my father's mother." The girl got slightly irritated and asserted proudly.

Latha became gloomy suddenly and said,

"*Achamma kadal kandittillya*." (Achamma hasn't seen the sea.)

She started scrawling something in the sand.

"Shall I help you dear? "

Latha denied Lachu's offer by saying it was a house unknown to Lachu. The contours of a house gradually became visible on the shore. The waves didn't wash it off for a long time. The girl didn't want it to be that way, either.

"Is Madam crying?" Adilakshmi's words suddenly diverted Latha's attention to Ammoppol, who stood far from them. There stood Kochoppol and a stranger with her.

"No, she never cries." It was Latha's confirmed belief about Ammoppol.

That night, Ammoppol didn't get back to the apartment. Latha learned from Kochoppol that she had left for Thanjavur for a funeral. A friend of hers had died.

The girl never spoke to Ammoppol. She had mixed feelings of shyness and fear towards her aunt. Perhaps because of her aunt's cold demeanor towards her. The sights and discoveries she had in the evening, made her night. That night, she dreamed of riding a white horse with a horn. She had dark glasses in it, and she was flying above the sea waters. Lachu and Kochoppol were waving their hands at her from the shore. But Ammoppol was still crying!

Rajalakshmi was mostly silent after returning from Thanjavur. She didn't sleep with them in the bedroom after that. Instead, she spent her nights inside the chamber near the bedroom. 'Lachu Akka was right', Latha thought, 'Ammoppol cried that evening, at Marina'. It even continued on the succeeding nights.

10:10 am, Ammoppol's apartment, Madras, 30 May 1989

It was the day of their departure. Lachu came late that day. She brought the *Panjamritham* (an auspicious dish prepared and offered to *Lord Muruga*) from the *Palani temple*. She had affectionately reserved some for Latha. Ammoppol had already left for the hospital, instructing them to get ready for the station by four in the evening.

"So, you are going back?"

Lachu's face was not so happy when she asked that. Latha, too, was sad. She told Lachu that her father might be shifting her to another place in the coming year. The child was worried, thinking that.

"Wherever you go, study well. All are not that lucky, dear. I don't even have an address to give you. We also have to move out of our area."

Lachu's consoling words ended up with her sighs. Latha didn't know what an address was.

Lachu made chapatis and peas curry for her. She gave her the *Panjamritham* and placed a pinch of *holy ash* on her forehead. They ate together. Kochoppol went to bid farewell to the neighbouring people.

Lachu made Latha stand in front of the mirror. She made her hair beautifully and decorated it with jasmine flowers, which she had brought in the morning. They made faces in the mirror and laughed at themselves.

"How beautiful my Charu is!"

Latha turned to Lachu, unbelievably.

"Can I call you so?"

The girl's eyes welled up. She stood silent for some time and then wept bitterly, muttering,

"Achamma and Kodi used to call me that. I want to see my father now."

"I know, your aunt has told me. Nobody has gone anywhere, and what if I call you Charu? Your name is as beautiful as you are! Charulatha! You will be back to your father soon dear." Lachu smiled.

The girl hugged Lachu, and then she noticed Ammoppol's unlocked chamber. Ammoppol had never left it like that before. From her gaze, Lachu understood what the girl wanted. With the hidden mischief, they entered the chamber. It was slightly dark inside. Lachu turned on the light, which was dim.

Everything about Ammoppol seemed flawless, and her chamber reflected the same meticulous attention to detail. The room was neat and organized. A simple cot lay against one wall, accompanied by a glass-topped study table, a chair, and a small almirah. A large iron trunk, painted in a hospital green, stood at the corner of the room, its presence almost imposing.

On the study table, several letters and diaries were scattered, but they looked worn and faded with age. Above the table, a collection of old photographs was carefully arranged beneath the glass surface. Charulatha leaned in, trying to make out the faces in the pictures. Among them were images of Achamma, Kochoppol, and Ammoppol, but the others were unfamiliar to her. Some photographs depicted Ammoppol with strangers—both women and men—whom she couldn't recognize.

"My father is not in this!" Charulatha mumbled to Lachu.

She went near the big box.

"How big! What is inside it, Akka?"

"Maybe toys for you!" Lachu smiled.

The word 'toys' brought immense joy to Charu's face.

In the dim light, up above the almirah, hung one photo frame of the youthful Ammoppol holding a little boy in her arms.

"Let's get out of here, Charu. Your aunt will come now."

Grabbing the girl's hand, Lachu turned off the light and left the chamber in a jiffy.

"Who is that boy? It's not my father. Sure", Charu was confused.

"I don't know. Listen, Charu, everybody has secrets. Some of them are confidential and should not be disclosed. It's not always good to dig. Only mean people do so. We are not so. Just leave it."

After packing dinner for them, Lachu came back to the girl with a photograph of them and handed it over to her, saying

"Keep this with you, Charu. Don't misplace it."

Both Adilakshmi and Charulatha were smiling in the photograph, as they used to do in the special mirror inside the bedroom.

❖ ❖ ❖

CHAPTER 7

THE FALL

'Unni, I know that mango tree in the south is for me. But don't cut it in my name. Never let anyone in this soil fall for me. I don't want it to be like that, son.' Achamma often reminded my father. Hardly could I make out what she meant then.

The rich aroma of freshly brewed coffee fills this cozy, air-conditioned room, wrapping around me like a warm embrace. The corners of this room are tastefully embellished with vibrant fake greenery, creating an illusion of nature's touch in this urban retreat. Delicate artificial vines elegantly cascade over the vintage portraits that adorn the corn-yellow walls. A polished copper vase, resting on the table beside me, cradles a cluster of bamboo shoots, their glossy surfaces reflecting the soft ambient light and promising a synthetic yet alluring shine.

As I savor my second cup of coffee, my eyes wander around, taking in every detail. I feel grateful for these glass doors that provide a window to the outside world. A dark wooden landscape unfolds just a few meters away from my table, with a magnificent tree standing out among the rest. Its lobed leaves rustle gently in the breeze. I am instantly transported back to that morning—a day that dawned without the biggest and brightest sun in my small universe. I was just seven years old when she fell.

A torrent of memories rushed forth from Charu, spilling onto the page.

❖ ❖ ❖

1988, April 10, Chittezham, Viruthi, Kerala

The breadfruit tree had fallen overnight. There were no storms, no winds, no sign of the impending fall. After sunset, the weather remained clear, with only a drizzle during her cremation in the evening. The night had been eerily calm. Yet, when morning came, the tree was down. It simply... fell.

Little Charu was fast asleep while her grandmother gasped her last. She went before dawn. Infrequent chatters roused Charu. She struggled to mount the threshold, which was half of her height. Her Achamma was wrapped in *'kodimundu'* (new clothing) there, and her eyes were half open. *'Why isn't she in her cot!'* Charu was baffled by the sight. There was a tarp raised in front of the house. The surroundings had a strange smell.

'Is this the smell?' She thought.

Three days back, a long-bearded old man, Nambeeshan, visited the house. He entered the anteroom with a thoughtful pause that resumed with the remark to Ammoppol,

"It's time, it's here lurking...I get it, Rajam."

The usual grit on Ammoppol's face faded with a twitch, giving way to an unsettled poise.

'Did he mean this smell!' Charu stood with a watchful gaze at Achamma's face. The old woman, Paruttiamma, had deep, dented patches around her eye sockets. People swarmed before Chittezham, and the girl could not make out their gestures. She silently sought the meaning from others and then looked inquisitively for her father.

There, the last of Parutty's children, her Unnikrishnan, stood shattered. His lean form was soaked in water after a few dips in the river. Grains of sand stuck to his wet feet and his limbs were clearly visible through the white *mundu* he wore. Water dripped from his hair, and his thin, precise moustache was slick with droplets. His chin trembled, chanting after the Brahmin priest. The priest told him to sit on the wooden plank and poured water from the *kindi* (One of the holy vessels used for doing *poojas* and rituals.) into his palm. Charu's father wiped his tears as he gave a handful of morsels to his mother. The ceremonial offering was made to the corpse.

That was not the first time the girl saw her father crying. He had been in tears for so many days after Achamma's fall. She had an accidental fall from the cot on a night. His eyes became wet whenever he approached Achamma's bed to clean her soggy cheeks. She had been bedridden since the fall. Unnikrishnan had instructed his daughter to keep Achamma's lips wet with a damp wick. She was happy at the privilege bestowed upon her. The chosen one!

Before her body was taken, everyone was instructed to lay prostrate at her feet, one by one. Charu and Kodi followed suit, though Charu stood there, uncertain of the ritual's meaning, feeling an odd sense of awe. In her mind, Achamma had always been a presence—someone who was meant to last forever.

The air was thick with the fragrance of sandalwood incense sticks, their smoke lingering in the room. The small cotton rice balls, set alight in open coconuts, continued to emit a rich, smoky aroma. It was then that Charu realized—death had its own smell. A heavy, dark scent that seemed to permeate the very air around them. Achamma was carefully laid upon the firewood, placed under the shade of the oldest mango tree to the south.

'Why would my father burn her?'

The sight made the child run to the spot. She wailed, calling her grandmother. At last, it was Kodi who took her inside to Kochoppol.

By evening, there was a slight drizzle. Kodi told Charu that they would never see Achamma again. Stories and mourns Charu used to hear from beneath the tattered blanket thus came to an end.

The only language the seven-year-old girl knew to express then was tears. There was nothing in front of her. Things were empty for Charu. For the first time, she slept in the house without Achamma, on the cot she had left empty. By midnight, the girl shivered with a high temperature.

The tree fell with a groan that night. People knew the inseparable bond between Paruttiamma and the surroundings of Chittezham. But that tree, at the southwest of the land, was Parvathy herself. It had held her memories, losses, pangs, and fragments of joy. A life that had been initiated and nurtured by her grew to ramify, hearing her whispers and mourns.

Every heart ached at the sight of it. Amidst the pain of one loss came another. Its huge trunk lay embracing the damp soil of Chittezham. Kochoppol used to say that Charu's first bath after birth was under the breadfruit tree. A tank was constructed under it, not so far from the well. Achamma would lay little Charu there in the *pala* (areca spathe), massage all over her body with turmeric, mixed in hot-processed virgin coconut oil, and then bathe her. This was a usual thing for Charu until Achamma's health was debilitated. With each kid at home, she treated the same.

That year on *Vishu*, there was no *Vishukkani* (the first sight of fullness and prosperity seen at dawn on the day of *Vishu*) set, and there was no Achamma to give her, the

Vishukkaineettam.

After Achamma's departure, the child spent her nights deliberating on those characters who were there in the stories told by Achamma. Paruttiamma used to tell stories of *the Ramayana, the Mahabharatha*, *Srimad Bhagavatham* and so many from *the Vedas*. Both Kodi and Charu listened to them eagerly. Among them, Charu was lured to the character of *Narasimham*. (The fourth incarnation of *Lord Vishnu*).

"Achamma, I love Him so much," Charu revealed a great secret that night.

"Who?" Paruttiamma laughed.

"*Narasimham*"

In return for the child's disclosure, Paruttiamma confided something in her.

"Charutty, you know, how I got Unni, your father?"

Charu turned to her curiously.

"It was in 1947. There was *Prahlada Charitham - Kathakali* (Presentation of the story of *Naramsiham* in the form of *Kathakali*, a classical dance-drama art form from Kerala) at the eastern entrance of Viruthi Shiva Temple. As He appeared, I prayed to Narasimha Swami and sought a boon from Him. I felt blessed by Him. That's how I got my Unnikrishnan."

She sounded emotional when she said that.

Kochoppol, who was lying down on a mat then, giggled at this description and asked,

"Amma, where was my father then?"

Achamma laughed at that comment and told her not to interrupt their stories.

Charu didn't understand what made them laugh. Her mind was full of the grand image of *Lord Narasimha Murti*.

"Did you get me in the same way, Achamma?"

Little Charu's voice was muffled against Achamma's chest.

"You are our little goddess, Charu."

Achamma planted a kiss on her gently as the girl asked,

"Will you take me to Him?"

"Sure, daughter, we will watch the play next time at the temple."

Charu always trusted Achamma's words.

Charu felt a bit jealous of the boy *Prahlada* in the story. That night, she vowed to herself that she would surely meet *Lord Narasimha Murti* and receive His blessings to get children in the future.

Little Charu had a series of doubts regarding certain character situations. She presented each of them to her Achamma to get them cleared. She asked if *Sita Devi* had pain while leaving her children; what would have been felt by *Ahalya* in the form of a stone? Why didn't *Draupati* have a female friend instead of *Krishna*, like Charu had Kodi?...

She went on asking, though her questions were mostly unanswered by Achamma. Once Charu shared her concern about *Devaki's* grief inside the prison.

"It must have been difficult for her. Poor *Devaki*!"

"Daughter, *Kamsa* was destiny, and *Devaki* was human."

Achamma's words reflected something that Charu couldn't comprehend. Her whimsical take on characters never dwindled with time.

Along with her Achan (father), Ammoppol, Kochoppol, and two of Achamma's nephews, Balu Ammavan and Sreedharan Ammavan (*Ammavan* in *Malayalam* means uncle), Charu also took part in the rituals. They took immersions and dipped half of Achamma's ashes in Viruthiyaru.

That day, a woman came home with a giant man wearing a cloth around his head. It was a *turban*. His beard was long, thick, and black. It was even longer than Nambeesan's. Their outfits were so strange. Charu had never seen such attire in the whole of Viruthi. The woman cried at the sight of Charu's father. He also grew emotional.

She spoke Malayalam, whereas the man remained silent completely. She called Charu near. But her shyness made her run to Kodi, who was in the kitchen. Kodi also didn't know who those strangers were. In Kodi's view, Charu's father resembled the guest woman greatly. They kept peeping at the man in a *turban* and shared their assumptions about him.

Kodi was fairly certain that he was not Malayali and added that she had seen such people on the train. Charu then wanted to know what a train was, which made Kodi scowl at her. Charu often confused others with her questions, and Kodi would often get irritated.

Kodi promised that one day they would go to Tambaram (a village in Tamil Nadu), where her house was. The guests were muttering something in front of the house. With her usual hospitality, Kochoppol invited them to join her for breakfast. The girls were still around the kitchen. 'Why are they not leaving!' Charu wondered.

Kochoppol and Kodi were busy in the kitchen preparing lunch for the guests. Ammoppol was inside her room. Charu waited for her father to come back. She had questions to ask him. With growing impatience, she went up to the *muchchu* (attic). It was a usual place where Kodi and Charu would share their small yet precious dreams and worries. They always felt safe in the attic, as nobody could ever find their presence there from down. During the rainy seasons alone, they couldn't occupy enough space there, as Kochoppol would lay provisions to dry.

Charu slouched and tried to play on the heavy wooden planks supporting the roof. Then Kodi came to place Achamma's spittoon up in the attic. Kochoppol had cleaned it and had told Kodi to keep it in *machchu*.

They started checking on those sitting there and could see Unnikrishnan and the two guests. A shade of happiness shone on Charu's face at the sight of her father. Unnikrishnan's beard had grown unevenly during those days of consistent rituals.

'Why hasn't he been shaving lately?' Charu thought to herself.

They were discussing something serious, it seemed. Charu's interest grew when she heard her name in their talk. The woman was forcing Charu's father to accompany them to Punjab.

"What's Punjab?" Charu asked Kodi.

"Ugh! Have you begun again? Kodi pinched Charu's cheek.

"We will play in the afternoon, Charu. Kochoppol wants you downstairs now."

Charu had lunch with the guests. It was then that Charu realised that the woman named Ambika was also her father's sister, and she had been married to that huge man in the *turban*. It all happened before Charu's birth.

Kodi didn't show up for lunch. Kochoppol called her many times. Charu went up to bring her. Kodi was sitting inside the *machchu* in a completely changed mood. She seemed to be unhappy about something. That day, Kodi didn't speak to Charu much.

Ambika and her husband, Surjit Singh, left in the evening.

"Kodi, that aunt has two names. One is Ambika, and the other is..." Charu had difficulty in saying the second name.

Kochoppol helped her by uttering 'Gurmeet Kaur.'

"No one in Viruthi has such a strange name!" Charu said with wonder.

"People of Punjab have such names, dear." From Kochoppol, Charu learned that there were other places like Viruthi.

Kodi remained silent while listening to their conversation. She gave an affected smile.

"Why did Achamma never speak about other places?!"

Kodi didn't say anything. That night, Charu slept with Kodi. Because she felt Kodi had some worries.

In sleep, Charu dreamed of Punjab. It appeared to her as another Viruthi, but with people wearing *turbans*. While Charu was asleep, Kodi gazed at her. She drew Charu's head closer to hers.

❖ ❖ ❖

CHAPTER 8

MALARKODI

Little did I know then, that the small secrets require you to pay a great price in life, someday. Maybe late or early. Somehow they might demand. I never wanted to have any. But, Charu had some... kept by others. All lips were sealed even before Kodi knew it. Nobody had got around to revealing it to me.

Charulatha pressed on in writing ...

❖ ❖ ❖

After Achamma got ill, Charu had to either sleep with Kochoppol or with her father. She preferred Unnikrishnan, as he was receptive to all her questions and mischief. She liked to lay on his chest, listening to him humming...

"Ammukkuttyammukkuttyaare pole.

Ummathum kavile vela pole.." (Malayalam folk song to pamper girl children)

She started asking him if they would be going to Punjab someday. She admitted to him that she overheard their talk the previous day. Unnikrishnan frowned.

"What you heard, Charu?"

"...that they want you to go to Punjab, will you take me also?" Charu asked.

Unnikrishnan's face showed relief, and he laughed by saying they might go there someday.

"Let's take Kochoppol and Kodi there as well." Charu reserved space for them too.

"Why not Ammoppol!"

She didn't respond to that. *'Achamma wouldn't be with us on the journey',* she thought.

Charu told him about what Achamma had told him about how she had got him after being blessed by *Narasimha Murti*. Unnikrishnan just listened to her chattering, but he seemed lost in contemplation.

'My house is like a banyan holding its boughs to welcome lives. Ambika chechi (The word 'Chechi' is addressed to older sisters in Malayalam.) knows it well. But she has changed a lot. She had been so different twenty years back.' Unnikrishnan's mind brimmed with emotions.

It was Koonanmavil Thomas who had brought the proposal for Ambika. He was working as a military cook then. Surjit Singh was his close friend. Thomas presented the matter to Paruttiamma. He told her that his friend, one Sikh, wanted to marry a Malayali girl. That time, Ambika was twenty. Kochoppol had already been married to Plakkoottil Kesavan Nair.

Paruttiamma was happy to entrust the girl if their horoscopes matched. Thomas convinced her that it was not needed from the groom's side.

"He just wants the girl. He has seen her already."

Ambika rarely visited Chittezham after her marriage. She and her husband were blessed with five children. On one occasion, she brought her three eldest sons to Chittezham, and Paruttiamma was content with her decision to marry Ambika off to Surjit Singh. *'At least she has a life now',* she reassured herself. But her concerns lay with Ammu and Kochu. Ammu had firmly refused to marry, while Kochu's marriage ended in disappointment. She endured multiple miscarriages, and her husband's immoral behavior ultimately led him to succumb to various health issues.

Kochu bore the pain silently, growing increasingly bitter toward men. The poor woman often found herself empathizing with Kunjikkavu, a character from the ancient tale of Chittezham. Through all of this, Charu became her world. Kochu raised her with warmth and love, alongside her mother. Meanwhile, Ambika's husband took Unnikrishnan to several places across North India. Unnikrishnan returned to Kerala after a few years and eventually secured a position in government service as a clerk.

Many months passed. Once, when Charu returned from school, Kodi was missing from the kitchen. Upon searching further, she found her inside *thekkini*. (Room in the south)

Her face had a special glow at that time. Kochoppol told Charu that Kodi would not play with her for some days.

“Kodi has become a big girl now.” She told Charu.

On the fourth day, Kodi got many gifts, including new clothes. She looked like an angel in her new red blouse and yellow skirt. Two years back, when she arrived at Chittezham, she was so lean and dark.

Charu recalled the day when she saw Kodi for the first time at Chittezham. It was an early morning in 1986. Charu saw an unfamiliar girl, around ten years old, in the kitchen. The girl was trying to push small pieces of logs into the burning hearth. The girl couldn’t reach the place properly and, therefore, struggled. It was she who smiled at Charu first. Her hair was dry without oil, and her eyes glinted in the flames.

From the living room, somebody tuned the radio, and a Tamil song started playing in the background...”*Padariyen padippariyen...*” Charu saw a few strangers in the verandah, enjoying the song by humming along. They were Kodi’s parents and three younger siblings. Their language had some similarities with Charu’s, but it was beautiful as a song. They called it Tamil. There were some words in it that Charu could make out, too.

It was Ammoppol who brought Malarkodi from Tambaram to Viruthi. Due to extreme poverty, her parents, who were coolies in Madras, couldn’t provide for their children sufficiently. So they had pleaded to Ammoppol to take one of them into her foster care.

But at Chittezham, Kodi had to remain almost like a child servant. Charu could never take her to school. Though Kodi was unhappy about leaving her village, she was happy at Chittezham for a reason, which she never disclosed to anyone except Charu. She feared returning home because of her *Mama*. (mother's youngest brother) She didn't like him. She was sure she would be compelled to marry him in the future once she reached Tambaram.

Kodi would cry, listening to Tamil songs. That's how Charu also developed a liking for songs. They never feared *Kalikavu*. They roamed everywhere at Chittezham, and during *Onam* season, they even went out in search of flowers, including the wild ones. They laid floral patterns in front of Chittezham and enjoyed swinging high on the swing Charu's father would tie to the mango tree. They made purses from cocoa leaves and took on roles as adult women, carrying those purses.

Often, they enjoyed meals together. Kodi would mix the well-cooked rice with coconut *chammanthi* on *ammikkallu* (a dry dish of coconut and spices ground on a grinding stone with hands), then knead it and feed Charu sometimes. She was no longer that shabby child. The geographical difference was so evident in her, making her extraordinarily pretty and plump.

On *Vijayadasami Day* (*Dussehra*), Achamma made Kodi write the Malayalam alphabet on the sand, spread inside the brass plate in the *pooja* room. She was a fast learner and became so proficient in the language.

Kodi was like a little guardian to Charu. She was very protective of everything at Chittezham. Once, she saw Charu sitting on the lap of a one-legged older man. He visited Chittezham with the hope of buying areca nuts. He had been almost a regular visitor there. The old gentleman owned many shops in the market. Kodi didn't like him. She hated his laughter, showing his tobacco-stained teeth, and the way he leered at females irritated her. He was a gentleman in Viruthi who garnered sympathy from others due to his infirmity.

Little Charu seemed to be uneasy on his lap. He was pressing the child's chest and other private parts while pampering her. The man was not letting her go. Kodi called her to the kitchen, saying Kochoppol wanted her there.

Charu never went to that man afterward. His eyes searched around for his easy prey whenever he visited Chittezham. But Charu hid inside the *machchu* at the sight of him. The child was worried, not knowing whom to tell and what to tell, which is what she experienced quite often from the grandfather-like man. Only Kodi knew what confused Charu, and she sat with her in *machchu* and told her,

"Charu, don't sit on that man's lap. Others might not understand. Sometimes, we cannot tell. He is doing something bad. No matter how tenderly he pampers you, he is not your grandfather. Even fathers are not good. In the village, Paatti (grandmother in Tamil) always says that men are strange creatures!"

Kodi wanted to say more, but she stopped there.

That year, after the *Onam* holidays, Charu received some shocking news. Ammoppol said Malarkodi's parents were coming to take her back in December. The child was saddened, and so was Kodi too. She was unwilling to go home and said she wouldn't have a happy life there.

"Kodi, we cannot own you from your parents, daughter. You have to go back to your soil, some day or the other."

Kochoppol was sad when she said that.

Each shade of protection was slowly getting lifted off from Charu. Achamma left. Kodi would leave soon.

Finally, the day came. Parents arrived to take Kodi. Charu and Kodi sat inside the *machchu*. They went on talking and playing until it was noon. Charu scattered her mini toys repeatedly, while Kodi struggled to keep them back in the bamboo basket.

"Don't go, Kodi. I want to play."

Charu wept.

"Charu, I want to tell you something,"

Kodi said after a pause,

"Sister, I have a secret to tell you."

The word 'secret' made Charu curious. But, even after many minutes, Kodi didn't say a word.

❖ ❖ ❖

CHAPTER 9

THE CALL OF THE SHADOWS

The succour and warmth those giant arms once offered were now dust. I felt breathless and started groping for something in vain. The tree loomed larger and larger, tapering the presence of everything around. It assumed a draconian form in the dark. A sudden gust of wind lashing outside made me cringe in a pool of dreadful misgivings. Achamma's thin fingers held me in a tight embrace. The child in me woke up with a start. A long dream that spanned thirty-two years...

That Charu was not at all familiar to me in fact. I remember how her nights were then. She was like a floating island that yearned to be a part of some mainland. But, she drifted off course, being so unsure of her destination. I can tell you how embittered she was then.

It was midnight. The nightlife in Thiruvananthapuram had come to a standstill since the pandemic hit the entire state. Charulatha had been in bed, preparing online presentations for her students. She suddenly slipped into sleep and woke up after the dream.

Even in March, Charu felt an extreme cold. She tried to reach the door, but her fingers couldn't remove the latch. She wanted to call someone for help but couldn't find her phone. The compression in her ribs and bones made her fear they might break soon. She pressed her face and shoulders in pain, feeling each spot ache. The streaming veins in her body felt like shards of glass. Overwhelmed, she collapsed to the ground in a panic. The thought, 'I am dying…' shook her to the core.

It wasn't the first time she experienced these appalling symptoms. With no access to a physician's help due to the severe spread of the contagion, all were forced to live isolated lives within their residences. After her father's death, Charu lived alone in her house. As the day broke, she somehow managed to make her way to Mumtas Manzil, her neighbour's house. Mumtas was a clerk at the University and was the mother of three.

Mumtas had noticed changes in Charu over the past few months. Despite her slight introversion, Charu used to be a cheerful and enthusiastic person. But everything suddenly changed. She stopped going online, ignored phone calls, and even avoided talking to Mumtas's youngest son, who was like a pet to her.

"What's going on with you?" She enquired.

Charu ignored all of Mumtas's messages and simply replied 'nothing'. Mumtas couldn't visit Charu due to strict measures imposed by the authorities and her husband's disapproving attitude. Additionally, her husband, who was working abroad, cautioned her against social contact.

When Mumtas last saw Charu, she appeared utterly drained. Mumtas suggested that Charu seek help from a physician, but her fear prevented her from doing so. However, Charulatha eventually reached a point where she couldn't bear the suffering any longer. She consulted a general physician over the phone, who prescribed certain medications, including antacids and probiotics.

Days passed, but Charu's discomfort persisted. She longed for peaceful sleep, but each twilight brought fear and unexpected trepidations that seemed like a formidable threat. Nightfall brought her cold sweats and palpitations, depriving her of any reprieve. Her eyelids grew heavy.

26 February 2021

The doctor accidentally caught sight of the woman in the waiting lounge while casually reviewing the CCTV feed. She appeared to be in her thirties and was deeply engrossed in scribbling something on a torn piece of paper.

Occasionally, she would dip in thoughts and then hunch to resume writing. Interestingly, the woman happened to be a friend of the doctor's acquaintance. Despite the regular consultation hours being over at his residence, the doctor decided to accommodate her. Being a renowned neurologist, he was recommended by her physician over the phone.

While waiting, she glanced at the name board displaying Dr. K. Suryanarayanan, MD, DNB, DM (Neurology—*PGIMER).*

The lady walked into the room carrying her handbag.

"Dr. Dinesh mentioned you. Tell me, professor, what brings you here?"

The doctor concurrently entered her details into the system as they conversed. *'Charulatha Chittezham, 39, female.'*

The lady took out a crumpled piece of paper and read her long list of symptoms in a feeble voice. She feared leaving any of her symptoms untold. The doctor attentively observed her mannerisms and body language, not entirely needing a detailed account from the patient yet allowing her to express herself. He reviewed her test reports, which showed no abnormalities thus far and noticed her hair displaying early signs of greying.

"What seems to be the problem, teacher?"

He asked, stressing the last word. The doctor smiled and looked at her. The woman sat mostly silent, at a loss for words to explain her condition.

"Nothing. I don't have any..."

She forced an artificial smile, amazed at why people kept asking her the same question. All the doctors she had consulted had approached her similarly.

"What do you teach?"

"Archeology", she said in a low vein.

"Oh! You people dig too much. Keep your shovel aside for a while. Is there anyone accompanying you?"

He inquired. She shook her head in response. The doctor prescribed a few medications for her, including multivitamins. He glanced at her as she stepped out of the room, visibly unsteady.

She pondered, *'Why did he make such a statement? Did he take pity on me? What could be the reason? Why did that person stare at me as if he had seen something bizarre? Is there anything wrong with me? Why didn't he say anything about my illnesses?'* She was completely baffled by these questions swirling in her mind.

The day after that, a small pleasure trip combined with a site visit was planned by her University College Department, where Charulatha had been teaching Archeology. She had been eagerly looking forward to this outing since the COVID times. She was the life of her department, bringing laughter wherever she went. Her presence alone energised everyone around.

It was a spooky night for Charulatha. The questions remained within her. *'He should have told me what's with me!'*

Despite numerous attempts, sleep eluded her. Her head splintered in pain. Her ears rang, and her arms tingled. An icy chill crept through her left foot, rendering her left side numb within seconds.

Alarmed, she rushed to the toilet multiple times, leaning on the wall with trembling legs. Her vision became blurred, and her stomach and heart drummed in sync. She felt a sea inside her abdomen, a boisterous one. Her breath struggled intermittently, and she started raving incoherently. She saw countless red and green eyes dancing in front of her in a single blink. She had a series of random visions flashing before. Even the sound of water drops dripping felt like needles in her ears.

Dreams were so common those nights. Strange black mist curled around the windows and crept towards her as if trying to possess her through her mouth. She tightly pressed her lips together, refusing to let it in. She desperately wanted to free herself from the stranglehold of that dark power, but eventually succumbed to death. What awaited her after was an esoteric calling of something. She saw her body being lifted to a corner, and it seemed to smile at her, as if proclaiming something incredibly blissful! Is this what they call death? If so, it's a euphoria like no other! unparalleled ecstasy! She wondered.

The phone kept ringing but she couldn't answer properly. It was Mumtas who called to check on Charu that day. She sounded exhausted. Mumtas sensed an uneasy air and reached Charu immediately.

"I wish there was someone here to hug me. I'm having trouble going upstairs because I feel like I might fall from there. I can't even eat anything properly, and taking a full shower is a struggle. I falter. Something strange is happening to me, Mumtas. I have no idea what's going on."

"I have an intense craving for sunshine. You know, I can't resist rushing out into the scorching heat of high noon. But then also, my body feels as cold as a stone. I long for warm afternoons, Mumtas. I can't stand the dark hours. They fill me with chilling nightmares. The idea of sleep sends shivers down my spine. It never happens to me. I catch glimpses of sights, but I can't trace where they start, where they go, or where they end. I sense the scent of death and despondency. I can't see any light. It's pitch dark, and I feel like I'm drowning in the depths of my river, completely alone and cold." She explained fearfully. Mumtas kept looking at her empathetically and placed her hand on her cold palms. Charu continued, her voice trembling slightly.

"Two nights ago, I had a peculiar dream about the banyan tree near the temple in my village, Viruthi. I'm unsure if it was just a dream or something else because I wasn't asleep at that time. In the dream, I saw dark and naked children standing beneath the tree. Those kids had messy hair. I tried to smile, but they didn't respond. Instead, they stared at me with a gaze that pierced my heart. Gradually, they dragged me towards the hole at the base of the tree. I screamed my lungs out, but no one could hear me. At that moment, I felt like I was being swallowed by an icy cold night. And you know what? That same tree fell yesterday in Viruthi. I got the news." Mumtas offered her some water from her water bottle. Charu gulped it. Mumtas said, "Keep talking to me and empty your minds." Charu continued...

"I witnessed a horrifying scene, too. A toddler girl relentlessly pursued by a group of wicked men. They caught the poor kid and straight up sliced open her belly while I watched. I tried to swoop in and save her, but I was way too late. I could see her crimson blood gushing forth. I failed to save her, Mumtas. Now, damn, these flies were buzzing around me, driving me insane. I tried waving them off, but those annoying pests just wouldn't leave."

Mumtas couldn't bear to see Charu in such a dishevelled state, so she held her tightly in her arms, deciding something in her mind.

❖ ❖ ❖

When Charulatha arrived at the clinic, she was completely blank. Her condition had deteriorated to the point where Mumtas made an appointment for her without her consent. Charu had no idea where she had been taken. *'Another episode!'* Charulatha thought to herself, a hint of frustration in her voice.

Charu glanced around at the unfamiliar faces with peculiar expressions. She looked at Mumtas. Her silence spoke of a war to Mumtas. *'Have I been brought to a mental asylum?'*

"Listen, Charu, just see the person inside the cabin. Try not to dwell on anything that upsets you. Relax."

Mumtas advised as if she could read Charu's unspoken thoughts.

'Maybe, my mind is not steady. Something is carried in me for sure. It stinks blood everywhere.'

Charulatha muttered to herself.

The days after that for Charulatha started becoming bright. The bleak gossamer of her impulsive thoughts was getting slowly cleared off, giving way to colourful rainbows.

❖ ❖ ❖

CHAPTER 10

REFLECTIONS

Hyderabad, 20 May 2001

Dear friend,

Today is my first wedding anniversary, and he is still the same. People say everything is going to be fine in the future. But where is the future? Life is utterly bleak for me. I don't have a present on which I can dream about my tomorrow. I think I may die of choking. Are all couples like this in this world? I don't have anyone to look up to among my relatives. Ammoppol lived spinsterhood. I never saw Kochoppol's partner. I have never seen my mother either. I don't have any friends too. Where can I learn the basics of marital life?

I thought I must befriend somebody who can understand me. That's why I chose you. At least I can share my...My pen slips with my sighs...

***

Three years ago, on Christmas Eve, in 2021, I retrieved my long-lost diary, which I thought I should leaf through. I did, too. It had very few pages written. The wretched girl in her twenties, in me, left them mostly unscribbled. Yet some pages captured her somber images in seclusion, sketched with charcoal and pencil. All of them resembled the pale petals of an autumn flower. Each blank page opened to those dark dungeons that breathed the tears of that lone girl.

What I write now cannot escape from them. They hold my reflections, which I couldn't complete then. But now I can do that to continue my story.

Marriage...such a sweet promise, an everlasting bond to be cherished. But for me, it was a haunting echo of shattered dreams and unfulfilled desires. A flurry of lies was waiting when I was thrust into that union, an arranged one devoid of love. With it, my aspiration to pursue higher studies remained a distant dream.

They wanted a docile girl, which I was. 'He too was gentle, innocuous', in Ambika Ammayi's (*'Ammayi'* means aunt in Malayalam) words. It was Ammayi who brought the proposal to me, and she put so much effort into making my marriage happen. 'See how lucky you are, girl! He is a well-settled boy with no family liabilities, and he is the only son of his parents. Your life is made, girl!'

After marriage, it was my maiden visit to Hyderabad. But I was surprised to find my husband's flat familiar. It was known to me as if I had seen the surroundings in some dreams. A shock wave passed through my spine. I had seen myself weeping inside the place.

As days passed, I realised how my dream had warned me of my future. Every single moment there was stifling for me, and I wept in the bedroom, in the washroom, in the corridor, having no one by me. I was often locked inside his apartment. He didn't want me to get acquainted with anybody outside. Sometimes I felt it was a protection. But it was never so. I was no Helen. I was just an average-looking, medium to dark-complexioned, typical girl of South India.

His hands shivered most of the time, and his mother's explanation of it was even strange. 'A cat killer's fingers always shiver.' From her, I got to know of a grave action of my husband that he had once killed a cat, with a single strike of a sharp stone.

No one visited us there, not even any of his kin. I felt like I was on a desolate island. I had never known scarcity, both in Viruthi and Thiruvananthapuram. But my husband's cheapskate behaviour granted me a meagre living.

With his inscrutable demeanour, he seemed like a stranger dwelling in the same space. Words never passed between us, and silence became our unwelcome companion. He dodged the burden of responsibilities, leaving me to bear the load alone.

On countless nights my pillow became my most attentive listener, often joining me in tears. A wall rose around me, my only comfort being my one-sided conversations with it. In those days, I realised that silence could be the deadliest thing and neglect the harshest form of torment.

I often wondered, 'When did I ever feel loved?' I was reduced to a beggar, forced to stand outside his room and sometimes outside the apartment. I waited long, for hours, weeks, months, and years, unaware of what had been happening between us. I internalised the belief that it was all my fault, that I must have somehow erred in his eyes or failed to align with his disposition.

I nurtured a sense of inferiority, feeling inadequate in the presence of others and the world around me. I didn't know if plants, animals, or humans perish without the living embodiment of love, but I believed I might. I didn't die though. The ache within my heart intensified with each passing day. I didn't know that I was being eaten by it, inch by inch.

I yearned for a child, a precious piece of love that could perhaps fill the void that consumed me. At one point, I devoted my days to worshipping the *Naga deity* at *Pambumekkattu Mana*, back in Kerala, even consuming the *holy oil* for twenty-one days as instructed, hoping he would be there with me throughout. However, it remained only my fervent wish. There was no one to share my feelings with. He could not grant me that cherished gift, no matter how much I desired I never felt it in him. I never meant anything to him. I was never, ever his need. I could see cliffs around me and my hopes just dashed upon them.

I was a spectator in a world that brimmed with happiness, standing like an outcast holding my desires to wait outside a paradise. I looked around me. There were happy couples blossoming in love's embrace. Their laughter and shared moments of joy presented a stark contrast between their lives and mine.

Once, I sought solace in the gentle guidance of a mind reader at a Psychic Relief Centre. A ray of hope flickered within me when I saw her compassionate gaze. But she revealed a harsh truth. She said he was an idiosyncratic character, a puzzle piece that did not fit the marital mould, a man who was obsessed with irrational thoughts. The weight of this knowledge shrouded me in suffocation, draining away the last traces of my optimism.

Society's intense stare trapped me in a cruel game of hare and hound. It thrust me with the responsibility of explaining my partner to others, convincing them of my plight, and validating my struggles. But he was always safe in his cocoon.

I wanted to be an artist, but those doors of opportunity I never cracked open with potential, remained firmly shut. I mourned the loss of my dreams, where the melodies of songs and the passions of colours once filled my soul. Marriage, they had told me, would be a gateway to new possibilities, an avenue to expand my horizons. But for Charu, tables were cruelly turned. The artistic fire within me had been extinguished, replaced by the cold embers of rejection and disappointment.

I never gave a clue to my father about how my husband treated me in Hyderabad. But, he could read the pang in my sunken eyes and presume my condition from the rare visits I made to him, unchaperoned by my partner.

My last visit to him was on the day of his retirement. He had mixed feelings of joy and sorrow. He cried, holding my arms, saying how he missed me. 'I wronged you, my child, I should have prioritised your education. I shouldn't have let you be like this. Never feel that you are alone. Achan is here for you. Don't get caught anywhere. Time doesn't wait for anything to be alright. Do what pleases you.'

My haven was soon to disappear, with my father's unexpected death. I remember it was a misty December morning when I received a telephone call from Bangalore. My father had gone there to attend a marriage function of his colleague's daughter. His body lay cold inside the hotel room. They said he died of chest congestion. At Chittezham, he was laid to rest where Achamma had been cremated. It saddened me that I couldn't meet him during Onam before he left. He had wanted me to reach out to him for some reason, but I couldn't get to him then.

I was heaving sorrows that swallowed me almost. I had nowhere to go and felt adrift in a sea of despair. They left me to ponder if that monotonous existence was all that awaited me. 'Will I forever remain a prisoner within the walls of this loveless marriage, doomed to watch as life passes me by?'

On one of my most confused nights, when I felt like the ground beneath me could give way at any moment, I realised how essential it was to choose myself above everything else. I didn't complain, but I spoke up, even if the other side was mute. I begged him not to hurl silence at me anymore. Not only were my feelings unreciprocated, but I also had to find myself standing all alone outside his apartment. My thighs were trembling, feeling the flow of menstrual blood. It was an unprepared night when I had my period. I realised what it feels like for a dog to have a door slammed in its face. But I tried to convince myself that he didn't hurt me any more than that.

The path was not clear to me. Yet, I decided not to return to where I had been banished. I had nowhere to go in Hyderabad. Numbness sailed through my veins. I left the place on the strength of the money I got from selling my chain.

I still remember how I thanked the train for sinking my whimpers amidst its whistles. I wanted to be back in Thiruvananthapuram. But Ambika Ammayi had already claimed my father's property by that time. She didn't want me to own a penny of his. I wondered why the woman hated me so much. I didn't have the least idea why she got into every scene in my life, especially between me and my father. It seemed she had reasons to claim my father's assets, which was not digestible to me. But, my father seemed to have forethought everything and had made financial securities in my name before he left.

I often recall Lachu Akka's words - *'Wherever you go, study well. All are not that lucky...'* I have seen the extremity of how desolate and desperate a woman can be without a vocation. I have also heard others express their disdain towards women becoming economically independent. They feared losing their women. They feared losing control over their partners and losing their sense of stability with their partners' horizons expanded.

My entry into the field of art and archaeology was never accidental. For me, everything around me has been an artefact teeming with timeless impressions. My younger days, spent at Chittezham listening to the stories, spurred my interest in digging up the backstories, and those evenings spent with my father at the Napier Museum and Park deepened that affinity further.

Gradually, I picked myself up. I grasped onto bits of hope, though they sometimes slipped through my fingers like fine grains of sand. Sometimes, I felt sadness that permeated every breath I took and ate me, leaving me to wonder again about my loneliness. I wanted time to respond to my queries, but as the sun rose on another day, I felt the weight of my grief pulling me further into the depths of longing, the irresistible longing of body and mind.

My reflections do not end here.

❖ ❖ ❖

CHAPTER II

THE FORBIDDEN DREAMS

And to say about dreams... They are like rivers. They carry us along, towards their tumultuous charms, ultimately causing chaotic churns within. Sometimes their calm charisma would carry us further to the cold folds hidden. There are times when a thud would be behind my middle upper back, warning me of something imminent.

My memory begins with a vague picture of me lying on somebody's lap. I was being fed, and my complete focus was on a toddler standing with a wide gaze. As I grew up, sights and visions changed. Sometimes, I experience a series of dreams that come to me while I'm asleep. However, what matters is that many of them stay and return, as if they were real!

If my memory serves me correctly, the first dream that occurred to me was when I was around four years old. That sight of an infant being abandoned by its mother and the baby's cries break my heart even now. After a few years, in the late 1980s, when television was introduced in our area, to my surprise, I saw the exact scene of the mother and baby in it. I couldn't sleep for many nights. I think I cried for days thinking about that separation. So what confuses me is 'Why do dreams happen to me in such a strange way?'

I always loved snuggling in my grandma's arms. Throughout my life, it has been a constant, bringing me comfort and security. I've always felt a strong connection to the females in my family and felt protected in their shadows. The supreme feminine embrace!

But, things changed. I've been experiencing unsettling nightmares, where ghostly shadows try to pull me into strange dimensions.

When did I transgress? I don't know. These dreams and eerie presence around me feel all too real. It all happened as if predestined. It's like it was meant to be, even though others might see it as phantasmagoric. But for me, it's not. It's my reality. My fall began that night...

It was a chilly evening in December 2016, when I finished sketching a self-portrait and decided to share it on Facebook, a platform I wasn't familiar with. I wanted to feel amidst others virtually. During my sleep, my tablet screen appeared in the middle of the night. Something flashed above my timeline - a name in the friendship request list. It read *Artist Agavan*. Since it seemed unfamiliar, I hesitated to accept.

But, for the whole night, for no reason, I got peeved with something and walked restlessly around for hours. Lately, I slipped into a light slumber and suddenly woke up with a jerk. I felt an intense rush of something around me and noticed a white fog approaching.

I tried to figure out what it was, but it wasn't a human. It had a lean, abstract torso with a translucent visage and shape. Although I was not familiar with the face, I was sure it had something to do with the masculine. Its limbs were long and were obscured by the surrounding mist. I could feel it gliding along my right leg and then upward, gradually making me think the heaviness of some real body on me. It was trying to occupy me and seemed to be in demand of something.

I was gradually swallowed by its impassioned energy, which wrapped me from all sides, and I wanted to break free from its hold. I fought hard to separate it, even if I couldn't grasp its form. It was intangible. I felt pressed up and down continuously and wanted to scream. Even after so many attempts, I couldn't make it. No sound came from me. I became breathless, and my heart was racing like crazy. I couldn't move my arms and limbs, and felt as if I were under a spell. All my efforts were in vain. It kept caressing me with hard kisses all over my body, and then entered me. Eventually, the bizarre encounter with the misty being turned me wet.

Once it left me, I regained strength to find myself panting in bed, all like a feather soaked. I tried to compose myself. What freaked me out the most was that it wasn't any dream because I was wide awake while all those quirky things happened to me. It was almost dawn, and I sat dumbfounded at the table. I couldn't even bring myself to look at my bed.

In the morning, I casually checked my mobile, recalling what I had seen on my tab. It was intriguing to find the same name in my request list - Artist Agavan! Startled, I immediately deleted it and carried on with my day.

Weeks passed, and one night, while I was sound asleep in my villa, the vision revisited me. This time, the name appeared and incessantly flickered, tempting me to investigate further. It was around 1 am when I woke up. I couldn't resist finding out more.

The same request was there again. The person's bio was the quote: *'I am Spirit, formless and free; whatever I think, that will I be...'* But, what caught my attention was the mention of Tambaram, which instantly brought back memories of Kodi to me. My curiosity got the best of me, and I impulsively accepted the request. That dawn welcomed me with beeps on my tab. I received a good morning message with the question, *'Can we be friends?'*

My apprehensions about males disappeared while talking to my father and the male gods. They had made my best boyfriends. But the entry of the new person brought sudden changes in me. It was a game-changer. Little did I expect that this new connection would completely transform my days, filling them with an inexplicable sense of excitement and butterflies in my stomach.

Time seemed to stretch on indefinitely as if refusing to pass by without him on the other side. His name was Agavan, a civil engineer from Chennai, and he sought a lifelong friendship with me. Although I longed to talk about Tambaram, his part often wended towards art and life.

He took a keen interest in the portrait I had painted and was particularly captivated by the eyes in the picture, making me take a closer look at it myself. While I had garnered followers for my artistic creations before, none had left such a lasting impression on me as he did. I had respect for the artist in him. How he philosophised life also was breathtaking.

I felt deeply connected to him, even if I had no idea how he looked. There was not even a single snap of him seen on his page. Despite that, we spoke informally, and I was comfortable with our casual exchanges. He was a married man with a son in eighth grade, and his wife was a high school teacher. The majority of his posts showed the desperate lamentations of a failed lover.

On our usual chats, he once sent me his family picture. I was flabbergasted at the sight of it. The man in it was tall, slender, in his forties, and he had the exact face of the mysterious, cloudy form that I had encountered that night in my room!

After this shocking revelation, I distanced myself from him for several days. I purposely ignored his messages and then blocked him. I just shut my account for weeks and withdrew from everything. But deep down, I felt the need to share the incident with someone. I opened up to Mumtas about my strange experience. However, I chose to hide a major portion of it from her. I couldn't tell her that the spirit had advanced to me physically, turning me on. I felt intimidated about confiding in her about the strange meeting with Agavan, too.

Mumtas, being a woman of spiritual call, I was sure she might provide guidance or offer clues to decipher the mystery. She took me to a spiritual healer named Janah, who ran a healing centre. Mumtas arranged a casual meeting to catch up on their friendship. The woman in her fifties observed me sceptically. She wore thick glasses. 'I have seen you somewhere.' Her tone was much firmer, and every word she spoke carried solemnity. After listening attentively to my explanation, she smiled and proceeded to her cabin, saying it could be some guarding spirit.

But, she soon returned with an altered expression and cautiously warned me about my relationships. 'It could be an evil thing, Charulatha. Don't be carried away. Beware while choosing dreams also.'

I couldn't understand what she meant. 'How can one choose dreams, Ma'am? Besides, it never was one.' She kept smiling at me. She seemed unconvinced by what I said and looked at me quizzically. 'Do you have anything more to say about how you experienced it?'

I didn't expect that question because I had been careful not to divulge everything to her. I briefly mentioned my previous experiences with predictive dreams. She winded up the session urging me to forget about these matters as if they were just stories. Afterward, she spoke to Mumtas in person while I waited outside. I couldn't help but wonder if the woman had somehow extracted anything from my mind.

While leaving the place, Mumtas invited me to stay with her for a few days, which I hesitated to do. By then, I was so preoccupied with the thoughts of Agavan and I started missing him terribly.

Consequently, I unblocked Agavan and got back to where I had met him first. He kept asking me why I had hurt him. It was evident that he had been waiting for me all those days, patiently. I didn't have a clear answer to his question. He expressed his emotional disturbances during my absence.

I asked him why he sought friendship from me and tried to convince him that it wasn't right to seek female friendship outside of marriage. I felt sorry for his wife, even though I was starting to develop feelings for him.

'Hey, stop preaching to me. I am not your student.' He kept reproaching me, saying it was a human wish to choose. 'It's all happiness that matters. I am distressed. Life under the same roof and in the same cot does not define marriage. I don't feel complete. I am living with a stranger. My wife thinks I am an ATM. She considers me useless. I want you. Do not see the world. It has its ways. Let it go. I am with my family only for my son, and you are my happiness; you are my medicine. Trust me.'

His confessional tone and how he texted, 'I want you,' stirred intense surges in me. I couldn't help but think about my past, about the one who had never wanted me for anything. I contemplated my Chittezham, pedigree, status, and profession. I am bound to all. How would I ever go beyond these?

But I loved Agavan, a feeling that had never happened to me at a younger age. Thinking about my fragility, I felt ashamed. I was slowly realising how much I craved to be loved. My body and mind desired that. I felt like fleeing to my childhood in Chittezham and wanted to fall on Achamma's lap.

Mumtas had constantly been forcing me to remarry. 'A lonely woman is always at the precipice, Charu. You have achieved so many things so far. That too through your perseverance. You have surmounted several hopeless situations. You are a fighter dear. Believe. It's time to settle, now,' she said.

She even brought a couple of marriage proposals from widowers to me, which I adamantly refused based on my findings. 'They might need female attendants for their kids. I don't want to be like that, and I cannot treat somebody's blood as mine. I can never own them with my heart.' I knew my outright denial upset Mumtas.

I couldn't imagine being in a life with someone again. Even the thought of it made me nervous to the core, reminding me of the trauma I had in the past. Marriage had never helped me grow. What I am today is all the result of self-help.

The label of 'divorcee' had diminished my value in the marriage market. And others said I could only have a second turn. But when did I even have a proper first turn? I have never truly lived my life, and now my age is collapsing. I am not worth it to anybody. It suffocates. Who was to blame for this? My father, Ambika Ammayi, or the society, or myself! It wasn't my fault. After all, I didn't elope with that man. It was never my mistake. It's pure fate. Even now, I console myself by junking everything to my destiny.

I am still not willing to belittle it as a silly dream. I had been unaware of what passion was and discovered it so late, at thirty-six. I firmly believed that it was his sensual passion that encircled me that night, nothing more, nothing less. The man on the other side had extraordinary energy to reach me from a distant place.

At times, I crossed *Lord Krishna* with my questions. I asked Him why he had devised such an episode in my life. Apart from all the confusion, I had a forced notion that Agavan was a true blessing. It was after he came into my life that I found true happiness. I was soaring far and wide exploring the romance in me. We would talk all day long, making the most of our leisure. During that time, my intense passion for art led me to create a cornucopia of paintings. It was like I was on cloud nine, experiencing pure ecstasy.

Once, he surprised me with a secret by confessing that he had been restless ever since he saw my eyes in my portrait, and he couldn't stop looking at it for several nights. That's how he fell for me. 'Charu, never show your eyes to anyone else. I might lose you,' he said. The word 'lose' saddened me. It made me imagine what would happen if he were to ever leave me. He became my everything. Even his temporary absence would make me feel anxious. I found myself stressed, thinking about how my loved ones had left me, one by one.

Once, I received a message from Mumtas asking me to meet Janah urgently. I had been baffled by the lady once, so I didn't want to get apprehended further. Still, I couldn't turn away from it.

Right from the beginning, her face showed a flash of a smile as if she had read my mind. After a brief reverie, she resumed to say, 'There has been a child in you, and she has something to tell you, Charulatha. Perhaps there's a secret, and you have to heal her. Whenever I try to connect to you, I get the image of a river. It was in my vision, too. And, one more thing. You have the grace of a goddess.' The woman's face was calm as she spoke.

The word 'goddess' echoed in my mind, bringing something I had forgotten. I tried to remain collected, yet a sea of questions surged inside me.

❖ ❖ ❖

CHAPTER 12

THE BURDEN OF SECRETS

The deepest of all depths in the world is perhaps the secret chamber inside a woman. It is like *machchu*, accommodating everything. Just like her mind, it is a silent onlooker in life. It embraces secrets, those dumped by others. It preserves dreams unkissed by the daylight and the night dews. And over time, a dark, misty cover might only remain. A promised asylum for bats and mice.

Love is a red oleander. You can adorn your hair with it, as Lachu Akka used to do. You can lay patterns with it on *Onam* days as Kodi and I used to do together. But never keep it close to your heart. You will be consumed.

Agavan and I engaged each other with our fanciful caprices. Our tale ushered in a multitude of wild dreams, which we secretly loved to believe were true. How would someone in love ever feel lonely? I wondered at the magical touch of the alien thing. I knew it was all a distant dream. Yet, I was all consumed in its passion.

My mind had been cluttered, the reason for which I could hardly mark in my therapy journal. The thought that I had been the cause for Agavan to cheat on his partner gave me agonising pricks. But the fear of losing him battered me more. Even after having prolonged sessions with my therapist, I couldn't vent out. Medication relieved my stress, and those strange moments of suffering got eased. But I couldn't let my love go. Thereby, I kept it in my arms safely like an inexhaustible melody. It still sweetens my cup of emotions, though unheard.

In Viruthi, my playmates teased me by saying that I had been brought to Chittezham in exchange for husk and that I didn't resemble anybody there. They sounded sensible. I didn't resemble anybody at Chittezham. It raked in too many questions for me. My consequent mistrust was often dismissed with laughter by my father. He did his utmost not to make me miss my mom. I could feel 'the mother' in him.

Whenever I asked about my mom, my father would go silent. I repeated my enquiry even on my last visit to him. I wanted to know how my mother died. No one, not even Kochoppol had ever answered my question. I asked Achan why he didn't marry again after my mother's departure. He remained calm. I wondered why he hadn't even kept a photograph of her! I wanted to feel her, at least in a frame, how I longed to be on her lap! How I needed to forswear my vexations there!

I recall him telling me a story about a woman from my girlhood. Everybody called her Adamma (*Adu* means goat; thus, it means *goat mother*). She was an insane vagrant who led a life grazing a small herd of goats. She had no name or land of origin to claim or own. She was dumb and free of all jargon, and her vernacular was always a smile.

Maybe the flood had brought her from somewhere. She had been searching for green pastures but, unfortunately, harboured an almost barren islet with some deciduous foliage. Her goats were happy, though. So was she.

Soon after reaching the place, she birthed a boy and died, leaving him in a pool of blood. Her blood became manure to the earth, and the soil frolicked like a lamb and welcomed the boy. He was the natives' final haven of hope and last reason to rejoice therefore they called him Hope.

A god's mother ruled the barren land. Her son god had left to conquer the thither world, which was more beautiful than the land hither. Hope was the only hope of his foster mom, and she raised him with her dreams and desires. With him, the land flourished. Nature dipped her brushes in the pitcher, where the mother poured her lullabies for her new son and stroked verdure across the landscapes. The bygone idyllic setting was thus restored. With its flora and fauna, the transformed land exuded the radiance of reassurance and faith.

Hope loved a nymph called Passion, whom he met by the green lagoon. He courted her for so long, but all his efforts were futile as she gave her heart to the celestial moon. Hope waited for her glance, overpowered by passions, but her eyes were always cast into the distant skies, and they gleamed like a full moon, lost in thought.

In the long run, all passion in Hope's heart drained, and he became incapable of performing anything. Still, he was like a god to his mother, so he needed to win over his passions. When agony struck him most, Hope would soar across the cloudscapes, where he dropped his tears.

Aeons passed. His tears rained down to form streams. They meandered through the land making it fecund. Over time, streams converged and formed a full river, brimming with life. It flowed towards all directions and those ripples touched the heaven's wide vaults. Angels from heaven took pity on Hope and sent a little angel to him with a mascot in hand. Hope found the cherub in a transparent chest that came along with the surges of the river. Hope's long waiting thus came to an end.

The narrative enchanted me, and that year at Viruthi Primary School, I drew its picturesqueness and won first prize in a drawing competition. The story moved me so much that it has never left my mind.

It was my second homecoming to Chittezham, after leaving Hyderabad. The house looked bleak. Those corridors remained doleful, bereft of any cozy symphony. It was an exact image of myself, all broken.

By then, Ammoppol's right leg had been amputated due to high blood sugar. She had an early onset of diabetes in her thirties. Never did she revisit Madras after her superannuation.

She was the only person who had been unhappy about marrying me off. Perhaps she had wanted me to have better prospects, but she had never expressed her concerns to me directly.

Ammoppol's room was small and tidy and reeked of allopathic medicines. When I was a child, I could never get there. We never had the permission to go in. She always locked the room either from inside or outside. It used to be like her secret chamber in Madras.

I stepped into the room doubtfully with a heavy heart. Her condition had been worse, and she was fully confined to bed. I tried hard not to cry in front of her. A face that had never smiled at me, an arm that had never held me, for the first time, they reckoned my presence.

'Char...' Ammoppol called me in a semi-conscious state, which I never expected. She was trying to say something in her decrepit voice. I stood heedfully to her, holding her palm. There was pain and helplessness on her face. She had arranged for a home nurse. The woman had been with her for many months. I felt sad about Ammoppol. All she had were lonely and indisposed hours inside the room.

Kochoppol was not there when I reached Chittezham. She had already joined her bedridden husband. The sick man used to weep as a child, the sight of which was unbearable to Kochoppol and she shifted to his place to attend to his needs. Her decision was shocking to Ammoppol, and she was thoroughly incensed by it. 'Women must not be this susceptible', she said.

I was happy that I could be there with Ammoppol during her final days. All that a daughter would do for her mom, I could do for her. I bathed her like a baby. Those songs I hummed to her, seemed to have relieved her malaises sometimes. But the kind of vivacity I used to see in that powerful woman never got restored. She couldn't even speak. Kochoppol made alternate visits to us. Although age had withered Kochoppol, she looked much happier while performing her wifely duties.

At times Kochoppol would sit by Ammoppol's cot. It seemed to me that she wanted to speak with her sister. And sometimes, in my absence, they made silent communications too. After all, the sisters had been shadows of each other.

Whenever I approached Ammoppol, she struggled to peer at the green iron trunk kept behind her cot by the wall. I had already noticed it when I entered that room. It had been with her since she returned from Madras, and we all used to call it *Madirasippetti*.

For me, it was an aide-memoire, that fetched memories of my childhood days spent in Madras, where I had found it. Lachu Akka, Marina, the mirror and the secret chamber flashed before me. I was sure it had never been like Achamma's wooden chest with closed compartments where she kept her betel box and starched *mundu* and *veshti*. (Traditional attire of women in Kerala)

I had never been curious to know what was inside Ammoppol's trunk. But the sight of it made me miss the trifling articles I had left in Hyderabad that night, which I retrieved later.

Maybe the trunk was like a strong room for her valuables, which she never wanted anybody to steal; a carrier of her solid emotions, which she never wanted others to surmise even. Perhaps, it held stories of affection, trust, sighs and sorrows which she never expected the world to know. I felt.

Everyone might need such boxes in life to lock up their secrets. I also longed for one. Sometimes, I wish my mind were a portable thing I could keep inside such a trunk whenever I needed it. But I did not know Ammoppol's trunk could be my pathfinder holding significant keys to a shady past. It had answers to all my questions.

❖ ❖ ❖

CHAPTER 13

THE CHOSEN

After Ammoppol's demise, Chittezham remained desolate like the lone youth in me. Nobody came claiming the soil. *'Not even a thief will enter here.'* Achamma used to comment casually with laughter. No one wanted to own the cursed land.

I had heard almost every story about the land from Achamma, and they never scared me as my dreams did. Chittezham had been like a haunted treasure island bequeathed to me. Each speck of mine carried its breath, blood, and memories. But back then, I couldn't realise how onerous the responsibility I had been entrusted with was.

I had wanted Kochoppol to stay with me then. I promised her that I would take care of her, along with my studies. And she came back to me after her husband's death. Kesavan Nair's final days of realisation had made him write his Will in Kochoppol's name. 'What will I do with all these? Nothing can I take when I leave this world.' Kochoppol was left bemused.

I took her to Thiruvananthapuram later, while doing my post-graduation, so I could fulfil some of her wishes then.

We went on a short pilgrimage. Her eyes were unparalleled in their calmness those days, and I would gaze simply into them. They were my best days until Kochoppol succumbed to a cardiac arrest. I had plans to gift her with the finest of things once I settled into a job. But she had left me even before I got my job.

Her evocative narration often filled in gaps in some of the stories that Achamma and Achan had left incomplete. On our pilgrimage, while at Chottanikkara Temple, Kochoppol mentioned a pentalloy locket that belonged to me. I was intrigued when she pointed out later that the locket had been kept inside Ammoppol's trunk. I never expected that Ammoppol would have something of mine in her possession. Her words gradually anchored me to the poignant portrayal of Kunjikkali. The divine girl had disappeared with her mom and an amulet.

Achamma's description of Kunjikkali had entranced me during my childhood. 'How would one be born without an umbilicus!' That thought struck me then, and I used to search for my belly button. 'Daughter, she was a saviour to protect her mother, Kunjikkavu.' Those words brought me to tears, thinking I couldn't save my mother. 'I shouldn't have had this on my belly!' I thought. 'Charu, you are the chosen one to save us. Saviour of our soil.' I couldn't comprehend what Achamma whispered then. Her utterances always ended in a guffaw.

The same day, Achamma told me that she had named me ceremoniously, and she added one more thing: 'You know what I whispered into your ear for the first time, Charu? I called you *Kunjikkali*, and I remember you smiled then. We both didn't have teeth.' What followed was a gale of laughter, revealing her toothless gums.

Maybe my skin colour made her say so. It took years for me to interpret her words in that way. But to her, I resembled the soul of the dark grove of Chittezham, veiled by the artlessly grown greenery. Therefore, she gave me the name *Charulatha*, which means 'beautiful creeper' in Sanskrit. I smiled, imagining Achamma holding me in her arms.

Once on my journey back to Chittezham, I felt the urge to probe into Ammoppol's secret trunk. Kochoppol had already consigned its key to me. 'Are the unknowns in the case significant to me?' I had the photograph with Lachu Akka almost unscathed, with me. I held it for hours, remembering that vacation I spent at Ammoppol's Madras apartment. But my mind stood confused in front of that secret chamber, and I didn't dare to enter it again. I wanted the company of Lachu Akka once again to do the invasion.

But I remembered her words, *'I don't even have an address to give you.'* It was immediately after that I felt the need for Kodi's address, which I thought I would never get. However, after much searching, I found it in Ammoppol's drawer. I did not understand a few lines because they were written in Tamil. But the last of the address lines was read in English, *'Thiruneermalai Road, Tambaram',* and I guessed it belonged to Kodi. I had an immediate longing to meet her. But the fear was so high on me, pulling me back from that adventure of going far beyond the borders of my land.

I became inconsolably dejected after having lost each of my family members, my blood. I didn't want to stay inside a house where I could see darkness and shadows. I left Chittezham in 2008. It was a sudden escape from the kind of monotony that had been taking hold of me. What I grabbed from there to Thiruvananthapuram were just three goods in my possession. Those things which had been shut forever with their owners' departure. They were Achamma's *Bhagavatham* book and wooden chest and Ammoppol's *Madirasipetti*.

But no deliberate distractions could save me from the impacts of vicissitudes. Moreover, the disasters of floods and the pandemic compounded each other to worsen my condition. I missed everything. I missed life. I missed myself. The thought that I hadn't lived yet grew in me alarmingly annoying.

After the course of my medication, I desired a departure from all my daily grinds. Those words of Ms. Janah recapitulated within me. I had been unmindful of her words and instead took them in abstraction. Not anymore, I wanted to lose myself.

Lachu Akka was right. '*...everybody has secrets. Some of them are confidential and should not be disclosed. It's not always good to dig. Only mean people do so. We are not so. Just leave it...*'

I am not mean, so I did not dig into others' backstories. That day, she said some stories are not to be told. But what about the other 'some'?

I must tell you, the other 'some' stories get revealed on their own. Time is like my Viruthiyaru. Just like her, it empathizes with you, reflects you, takes you with its flow, and gets you lost in its intricate depths. It is even more detrimental to reach the confluence. Perhaps it's not good to meet another river. Your course may need to be altered, culminating in an inner crisis. A total loss of distinctiveness!

That's what happened to me after Agavan's arrival. I had been a river that took a wrong turn at its origin itself, and that truth I had been blind to. The journey to it imprecisely began with him. And it gained ground due to his place, my Kodi's Tambaram.

It had been thirty-three long years since I had visited Madras. On a sweltering day in April 2022, I arrived at Chennai railway station. And that Madras was missing there when I disembarked. I had a vague idea about how the place might have changed. Still, I was astounded by the diverse changes that ultimately took hold of the land.

Agavan stood waiting for me on the bustling platform, and my heart raced at the mere sight of him. For the first time, I was meeting my love, and the sheer intensity of the moment left me breathless, my eyes shimmering with tears. Slowly, he removed his dark glasses, and our eyes met. Yet, I restrained myself from reaching out—not even offering a handshake—as I was deeply aware of the boundaries that defined our relationship.

He had thoughtfully arranged every detail for my comfortable stay between Tambaram and Chennai. Throughout our time together, his joyful presence provided warmth and reassurance, mingling respect with genuine compassion. His carefree spirit dissolved my anxieties and gently removed layers of inhibition, leaving me more poised and serene. In his company, I found an unexpected refuge—an invaluable respite from all my lingering uncertainties.

We visited the area where Kodi's house should have been, as per the address. However, those lanes had been demolished, and buildings had taken their place. Her house was not to be found amidst the edifices. Before I arrived in Chennai, Agavan had already warned me about how difficult it would be to locate the address and how markedly Tambaram had changed over the years. He sought the maximum ways to find her.

As days passed, my hope waned. But Agavan was unresigned and he resumed the task indefatigably. He prioritised my happiness and took me to beaches and temples in the evening where our moments were incredibly memorable. Even the blazing summer heat was soothing to me, and I felt myself reborn in his presence.

Days slipped away. I couldn't avail of any more leave and had no time to stay back further in Chennai. There was no hope of finding Kodi. Yet at my hotel room I kept reassuring myself not to lose and that I would definitely meet her soon. Just two days before my departure, Agavan called me,

'I have a surprise for you, Charu. Get ready by noon.'

He sounded rejoiceful on the other side.

'We have a drive towards Mahabalipuram.'

The place sounded interesting to me. Its archaeological significance was well-known to me. Before noon, he came to pick me up, and we set out on our journey. We started moving through Chengalpattu.

He said nothing even if I asked him what we were up to. I was in the grip of excitement, but, in tandem, something worried me throughout my way. 'Why is he taking me towards Mahabalipuram instead of Tambaram?', I wondered. But I trusted him like the dawn. We passed the junction and took a turn onto the highway. The road teemed with vehicles.

I was sitting to the left of his seat in the front. He asked me while on the drive,

'What if you meet Kodi?'

'I will take her to my home. Are we to her?' My reply was abrupt.

He turned to me with a smile,

'What if Kodi were unable to shift to your place?'

He continued after a pause.

'What are you going to achieve from this loneliness, Charu? I cannot marry you. But I want you with all your willingness. And I will not force you for anything. You have asked for my wife. I will take you to her. She will be back from her mom's place tomorrow.'

I couldn't utter anything and eluded his gaze to my left. The mirror in front of me held the image of a middle-aged woman who bore too many unfulfilled dreams and turbulent emotions. I felt frozen in the air-conditioned car, so I held my palms together.

'Are you okay?'

Right then, I felt his clasp on my arm, which was warmer than the high noon sun I used to crave and that used to hug me on my woebegone days. I shuddered at that touch. My discomfort made him stop the vehicle. We had just passed the Singaperumal Koil road.

'Hey, relax. Nothing will harm you.' He continued after a pause. 'Let's have something from here. Come out.'

He crossed the road, aiming at the tender coconut seller.

I feared touching him. Still, I wanted to hold his hands and stand in his embrace forever. Though he defined my happiness, I suffered amidst the ethical dilemmas. As I watched him buy the tender coconuts, there was a sudden throb of pain in my head. He was smiling at me throughout as he crossed back to me. In pain, I smiled at him. Before he could reach me, in a split second, Agavan was run down by a speeding car. I heard screams. Everything went mute afterward. I could see blood and the beating sun, which dazed me. I slipped into darkness.

❖ ❖ ❖

CHAPTER 14

THE FORSAKEN BOON

Twilight settled heavily upon the land, casting its mysterious spell over the Viruthi Temple Hall. The air vibrated with the thunderous presence of an otherworldly figure, illuminated by ethereal streaks of celestial glow. Gradually emerging from this mystical ambiance were characters adorned meticulously in their traditional *Kathakali veshams—Pacha, Kaththi, Thaadi, Minukku, and Kari*—each embodying their unique traits through vibrant attire and intricate makeup.

Yet, amongst them all, the majestic form of *Narasimha Murti* stood apart. With His fierce white mane and elongated, gleaming nails, He commanded attention amidst the golden radiance flowing from the *Nilavilakku*, a sacred lamp positioned reverently on the floor. As He emerged through a veil of shadows, accompanied by spirals of holy smoke, His measured footsteps synchronized perfectly with the rhythmic crescendo of the *Melam*—the grand musical symphony produced by traditional instruments such as *Shankhu, Chenda, Maddalam, Idakka, Chengila, and Ilathalam.* The spectacle resonated deeply within every spectator's heart, heightened by the lingering fragrance of incense, camphor, and the smoky scent of flickering torches.

Little Charu sat spellbound among the audience, gripping Achamma's hand tightly as *Narasimha Murti* made His dramatic entry. The crowd stood instinctively, their voices blending into a fervent chant of *'Narayana...'* Tears filled their eyes, yet Charu remained transfixed, her gaze unwavering upon the captivating creature before her.

With fierce grace, the deity tore apart the demon with His powerful claws, settling afterward with palms dripping symbolic blood. Every story Achamma had once narrated sprang vividly to life before Charu's astonished eyes. Entranced by the ecstatic drama unfolding on stage, she instinctively moved forward, leaving Achamma behind, yearning deeply to be held by Him, just as the little prince *Prahlada* once was.

Before retreating, the deity's gaze fell upon Charu. Raising His finger gently toward her, He beckoned her closer. Silence enveloped the hall, soft as still water, as she slowly approached the awe-inspiring half-beast. "Hold me..." she tried desperately to whisper, but the words stayed locked within her throat. And there, lost in overwhelming splendor, Charu forgot entirely to voice her heart's most secret wish.

The *Lord's* eyes sparkled as He beamed at the girl. The girl seemed fearless though.

"Save him"

Little Charu beseeched, gesturing towards Agavan lying in a puddle of blood.

The atmosphere became resonant with the *conch call*. A blood-smeared palm drew closer to Charu. It gently patted on her forehead and then on her cheek. At the divine touch, a tingle of horripilation dashed through her. The girl bawled her eyes out, grasping His arm.

As her glance caught on the Lord's sacred countenance, His third eye slowly fluttered open. Red waves were lashing inside it, and amidst them emerged an image of a dancing female *Oracle*. She was dark like the darkest of nights in the month of *Karkkadakam*. Her hair was untamed, and, with each move, jingled her golden girdle and anklet. The sword she held was stained with blood. Charu, who stood fearless until then, felt a sense of dread inside.

"*Kali...Devi...*" (Goddess)

The girl intoned.

Charu tried to discern the enigmatic figure before her. The figure gradually stepped towards her. Her tresses were like black cobras, hiding her identity.

A shriek escaped Charu. What was unveiled in the eye was her reflection. Blood trickled from the *Oracle's* forehead and tongue, daubing the face of the little girl. Charu screamed out for Achamma.

'Ma'am...' A call continued to ring out, piercing her ears. Charulatha opened her eyes. Neither the *Lord* nor the *Oracle* was standing by her.

"*Njan evide anu*?" (Where am I?) She asked herself.

"*Neenga Malayali ya*? *Ipo neenga pathukappa irukkinga Madam...Kavala padathinga*." (Are you a Malayali? Right now, you are safe, Madam. Don't worry.)

A voice came comforting her.

She looked around dazedly to make out where she was. It was a hospital. There stood a nurse who had been calling her frequently from her ramblings. Charulatha felt a heavy head, which had been bandaged, and her pillow had spots of blood.

"You fell, Ma'am. But, nothing to worry about. It's a minor injury."

Charu listened heedlessly to the nurse describe what had brought her to the hospital bed. She remained unperturbed and calm until she regained full consciousness. Soon, she became alarmed by the thought, 'Where could Agavan be?'

"What's with him? Where is he? I want to see him. Please tell me, Sister."

"Be relaxed, Akka. His condition is critical. He has internal bleeding and has been taken to the Neuro-ICU. You cannot see him now."

Charu didn't say anything for the succeeding seconds. Her heart began pounding inside her ears. It was dark outside the window. She was oblivious to the time but noticed the wall clock, which showed 8:20. Nobody she knew in the new place, except Agavan. 'What could be his condition?'

She kept her palms closer to her chest and recalled her unprecedented vision: *'I met Him. Still, I missed asking for it!'* The wish she had kept since childhood remained unfulfilled.

Time crept by...

Awful silence settled over the corridors. Charulatha staggered along, intending to reach Agavan. After a painstaking search, she finally got near the ICU. The visitors' room along the verandah was not crowded then. She identified the lady who had been sitting in the first row. It was Agavan's wife, Poovizhi, whom she had seen in his family snaps.

The woman looked crestfallen. Tears had stained her cheeks. Charu approached her, fumbling for words. She raised her eyes at Charu.

"Was that you with him when he drove?"

Someone from behind made an abrupt inquiry that Charu didn't expect. It was a middle-aged man who spoke.

"Yes. I came for his help in finding someone here. He was hit in front of me."

Charu struggled to be steady.

"I am Senthil, Agavan's cousin. The phone inside the bag had a picture of you. That's why I could identify."

Senthil was Agavan's workmate, too. He handed the handbag to Charu, which she had left in Agavan's car. She learned that Agavan had been taken to the Operation Theatre for a medical emergency and would be complex hours for the patient and family.

"Doctors say he has...he has a lower chance of survi..."

The man couldn't complete it.

Mournful weeping was heard from behind. It was then, indistinctly there, that Charu spotted a group of people who had broken into tears. She remained dead, unable to console anybody. The sight of the whole family whisked her hard, and she foundered in the chair. A sense of guilt and self-loathing smothered her.

'Family, the most precious gift that I lack right now! How mean I have been! No, I cannot put my own interests ahead of others' lives. My desire and dream cannot be fulfilled upon somebody's aspirations. Nothing can harm him. I cannot let that...'

Charu, composed yet on twinges, turned to Poovizhi and whispered calming words.

"He will be back to you. Nothing can harm him."

All Charu wanted for herself was reassurance. She asked for Senthil's phone number.

Moments drifted by...

The phone rang continuously, breaking the dead quiet in the waiting lounge. It was Mumtas on the other side. Charu hobbled towards the elevator with her phone.

"Is something wrong? Why haven't you picked up my call, Charu? It's past midnight?"

Mumtas sounded uneasy. Charu quivered as she spoke. She strained between what she had hidden and what she felt compelled to reveal. There was an anxious pause from the other side until Charu finished.

"Why are you after this? It's all misadventures, Charu... Why would you suffer searching for an old playmate? See where you are now! Come back."

"Where have you been, Ma'am?"

It was when a senior nursing staff approached Charu with a gruff voice.

"I will be back in two days. I will call you in the morning."

Charu hung up. Her mind was crammed with the thoughts of Agavan.

The day broke early. Sunlight filtered through the window, throwing patterns on the sill. Charu remained motionless in bed. Her eyes were sullen, deprived of sleep. But despite the woes, some distant hopes still lingered within them. Thrice, she went to the duty room hoping to get some news about Agavan.

'Should I call that man?'

She searched for Senthil's number, but soon left the idea. Her focus shifted to her mobile. Time seemed to be still.

One junior staff member informed Charu that she would be discharged by noon. She stood in the corridor, looking at the distant sun. The day was progressing.

A voice stirred her from stupor. It was Senthil. Charu passed a half gaze at him.

"Surgery is complete. He is out of immediate danger."

Saying this, Senthil heaved a sigh.

"I knew this."

There was sunshine on Charu's face as she said it.

"Nothing can harm him. He is back. I knew this. I waited for this. I can leave now."

She muttered to herself, wiping a few stray tears.

"Can I see him?"

"No."

Senthil glared at her in disbelief. Her quick shift in response and moves surprised him. He watched her walk briskly, resolved to reach Agavan.

❖ ❖ ❖

CHAPTER 15

THE TAMBARAM NOTES

The afternoon rain ebbed away amidst lingering echoes of thunder. Deep, monstrous rumblings reverberated through the sacred soil of Sree Padmanabhan—the hallowed land of *Lord Vishnu* known as Thiruvananthapuram. It was the serene month of *Thulam*, third in the Malayalam calendar. A sudden thud from the backyard jolted Charu awake from a restful siesta, abruptly ending her leisurely Sunday repose.

'Must be the street vendor again. My hospitality has spoiled her so much that she's mastered the art of arriving precisely at the most inconvenient times. Enough!'

These thoughts echoed in Charu's mind as she jolted awake, unsettled, and stumbled toward the door.

"Still, this just won't do," she murmured.

Restlessness stayed heavily within her. Another sleepless night had passed, and fatigue clung stubbornly to her drooping eyelids. Charu swayed slightly as she made her way first to the front, then toward the backyard, only to find it empty, save for a few birds. The premises weren't an exact replica but rather a smaller imitation of Chittezham—a design both father and daughter had intentionally pursued within their modest living space.

Occasionally glancing back at the gate and neighboring houses, her eyes fell on Mumtas's home situated near the road's bend toward the junction. Mumtas had already flown off with her children to join her husband in the Middle East.

A sudden, peculiar screech welcomed Charu as she approached the star fruit tree. She craned her neck, searching until she finally spotted a parrot blending seamlessly with the lush greenery. The bird adeptly removed fringes from the fruit, delicately accessing its flesh. The vivid green stood out distinctly against the damp foliage, still glistening from October's cleansing rains. A swift shake of the branches splattered droplets onto Charu, bringing bumps on her.

Thulam's rain clouds hung low, gathering strength as they drifted westward from the east. The breeze carried with it the heady fragrances of elengi and nutmeg. Cranberries blushed vibrantly while pepper vines danced in the wind. The garden's glow remained subdued without the watery sheen of seasonal Rose Apples. Even the betel leaves seemed forlorn, missing their usual visitors.

"At least the betel leaf seller who keeps a stall by the temple might have shown up!" Charu sighed aloud.

"No one ever comes here anymore. Perhaps my touch could comfort you," she whispered, moving toward the betel vine. Stretching out her arm, she carefully plucked three leaves. A familiar rat snake swiftly emerged from the bushes at her approach, hastily slithering into its abode amidst the nutmeg tree branches.

A pile of coconuts lay pulled down from the tree near the tiny log cabin. Charu collected a handful of coconut fiber, preparing for her nightly bath.

'Tonight I might sleep...' She sighed.

Everything came to a halt for Charu since last April. Nothing could engage her slackened spirit after Agavan's accident. She became much pulled down with each day. And was hopelessly hopeful, those days, battling to calm herself down.

Lonesomeness was never new to her. But deliberations on love and loss tossed her into the chaos of depression. Finding ways to escape those testing times was a challenge to Charu. She avoided medication but attended therapy sessions occasionally. However, she never shared her incident with Agavan with her psychologist and opted to remain closed off, like a vault, after the incident.

Charu's wish to see Agavan after the surgery remained unfulfilled as she had been denied permission. Heartbroken, she had to return to Kerala. Often, she would call Senthil and be informed of Agavan's condition. But she never dared to call Agavan's number. The thought made her compunctious, and she felt responsible for the accident he had met with.

Agavan had been hospitalised for two months, completely unconscious. He suffered multiple contusions and sprains. The left half of his face had been torn apart. The facial trauma had to be fixed through plastic surgery, while he lay dormant. His family had been through severe hardships since then. They had sleepless nights and days attending to him.

The post-traumatic phase altered him dramatically from a gentle to a rough, hot-tempered person.

'He is no longer our buddy now. He has become a badmouth and has grown much more irritable. He doesn't even let the physiotherapist near him. We have to hold his arms and legs for the sessions. It's painful for him and us. He yells at everybody and is so obsessed with something. We cannot contain his abnormal anger and stubbornness. You know, he hates everything and has started doubting Poovizhi too. Poor thing... Doctors say that such violence is normal after certain neurotrauma. It might get abated with time. But gradually only...little by little. With some, there is no cure. It lingers for a lifetime.'

Charu recalled Senthil's words again that evening.

'I wish all my memories would just fade away!'

She stayed too long under the shower with her eyes shut.

After the sumptuous bath, Charu sat meditating. Thereafter, she lit the twilight lamp, cleaned her Achamma's betel box, disposed of a few dry betel leaves, and placed the freshly plucked ones inside. Soon, she resumed her canvas and colours.

The rain replayed its melodies before nightfall. Charu took her mobile phone to turn off the flight mode. A list of missed calls from an unknown number was displayed. Mumtas had also sent many family clicks.

Agavan's name appeared on the call list, piquing Charu's curiosity. She attempted to return the call, but it didn't go through. Then, she noticed Senthil's message:

'Someone has been calling Agavan's cell. However, today only Poovizhi answered. A woman from a village near Mahabalipuram was on the line. She asked for your number—you're Charu, right? Poovizhi provided her with your contact. The caller wanted to share this with you, but she couldn't reach you, so I'm passing along the information.'

Charu felt a chill run down her spine.

'Mahabalipuram! Who might that be? Where was Agavan taking me that day? Senthil said she asked for Charu. Is there somebody who knows me?

Water dripped from her curls to wet the mobile screen, which she tried to clear several times.

'The other number...'

She looked for the unknown number and tried calling it. A female picked up the phone on its third ring.

"*Charu va*?" (Is this Charu?)

There was complete silence for a few seconds.

"*Athe. Ningal aaraanu*?" (Yes.Who are you?)

"*Neeya enna pakurathuku ivlo dhooram thandi vantha?*

Ipo enna itha mathiri kelvi kekura?" (You only came too long searching for me. Then why are you asking this way now?)

"*Charu, Kodi dee... Enne ariyille*?" (Charu, it's me, Kodi... Don't you know me?)

The short stillness suddenly turned into a low wail. The two women had stories to tell of the long thirty-four years. Yet, a stifling silence hooked them up.

In the ensuing moments, both Charu and Kodi relived their childhood. Charu caught a whiff of Chittezham around her. Years of angst made her so impatient that she longed to see Kodi then and there.

"Where are you, Kodi? I have been searching for you. I want to see you now."

"Charu, I will give you another number to video call. But now, I can just make voice calls using this. That, too, is not always possible."

Kodi's voice dropped suddenly to a murmur.

"This night might not be sufficient to tell you about me, Charu. What about others at home? And how are you, Charu?"

Kodi wanted to hear about everybody at Chittezham, and each description Charu gave fell into the keening wind.

"Can you get back to me? I have lost everything. I miss those times when we used to be together. Please come back. I am coming to you to Mahabalipuram."

"No. I am not there. And you should not visit me as well."

Kodi's tone was rather emphatic.

"Time is short. I cannot wait for anything. I don't, either. I waited for you that day. But you didn't show up. That man, to whom I had spoken, too, didn't respond to me further. He had told me how difficult it had been for him to locate me. He said one friend from Kerala had come for me. I mentioned your name, and he smiled. That's all. Didn't he say anything about me? How do you know him, Charu?

The zipped-up tale of Charu's love is thus revealed to Kodi.

"If he hadn't been there, I wouldn't be talking to you like this, Kodi. But maybe he shouldn't be with me. Destiny has fought tooth and nail to defeat us. We are star-crossed. And I feel, it's all because of me. But it happened..."

Charu went eloquent about Agavan, and her shelved sorrow gushed forth.

"Even I am thankful to him for getting me to you, Charu. But dear... I cannot visit you or let you to me."

"But why? What stops you? I see a complete void here. Can I come to you at least once? I would like to meet your family and your children. When did you move to Mahabalipuram?"

Charu's voice was growing impatient.

"Charu, it's not exactly Mahabalipuram. It's a few kilometers away from there. I had to shift to the place. But I am not there right now. My marriage was arranged with my uncle. But I didn't marry him. I displeased my parents by joining another man, and my uncle married my sister. But..."

Charu became silent while listening to what fate had in store for Kodi.

Just before her wedding day, Kodi eloped with Arputharaj, a lorry driver whom she loved. Thus she brought dishonor to her family. But the man turned out to be a cheat. To him, Kodi was just one of the prey. He kept multiple sexual partners while married to Kodi. He set marriage as a means to ensnare women just for the sake of money and pleasure.

Kodi was blind in love. She placed absolute trust in her husband. In due course, she gave birth to a girl. Even after realising Arputharaj's sham love, Kodi had to stick to him. He sought different ways to make money but never supported Kodi financially. Life became wearisome for her. She remained helpless and had to resort to laborious tasks to make a living.

Abhorrence brewed up in her when Arputharaj forced her into prostitution.

"I was never ready to do that. He often borrowed huge sums from people and sent clients to me. I had nowhere to go, Charu. He was more than a sadist. I was raped in front of him, and you know, he was enjoying all my pain and cries. Your Ammoppol had invested some money in my name. That monster looted that, too."

There were sobs from both sides as Kodi spoke.

"I became a garbage can. Even my tears are tainted, Charu. What should we call a man who sells his wife? A pimp? No, right?"

Kodi reminisced her dark days when Arputharaj used to lock her inside a room with her daughter.

"Why couldn't you escape? Couldn't you seek somebody's help?"

Charu fumed with anger.

"I tried. But he was like a henchman and had connections with many influential people. At times, I wanted to put an end to my life. But my daughter's face pushed me back from the thought. He was unfeeling towards us. My child never got her father's attention until she passed her girlhood. And that was the final straw for me. That animal touched my girl lustfully saying that it was his right to enjoy the fruit of his labour. And I decided..."

"What?" Charu felt jumpy.

"He got killed in an accident that month, after the *Thai Pongal* (the harvest festival of Tamil Nadu). People say he fell from the train while travelling with his friends. He was drunk. I boarded a train just once, after my return from Kerala..."

Kodi paused in unrest and continued.

"... and it was on the same day of his death."

"Did you...?" Charu sat breathlessly.

"Charu, you have always been my darling sister who loved stories. But, don't you still know that some stories do not invite questions?"

Despite the pain, Kodi chortled.

"He used to keep us on the Andhra border. My daughter was fourteen when we fled back to Tambaram. But all changed by then. My father had died years back, and mom had shifted to my sister's house. She had been bedridden for two years. Last year, she, too, passed away. I wanted to forget everything that had happened to me and hoped to get healed for my daughter. I started working with an agency recruiting home nurses near Mahabalipuram. But, Charu, the phantoms of my past raven my present, bit by bit. I have been defiled."

Charu had questions to ask. But Kodi's woeful life journey made her inarticulate.

"We had been at a government-run service home."

"Are you not together now?"

Charu became nonplussed.

"We are not. I cannot stay there. I am a carrier and patient. I am infected with HIV."

❖ ❖ ❖

CHAPTER 16

CHILANKA: THE BONDS OF BLOOD

It was a warm evening in March 2023, and the Museum Gallery buzzed vibrantly with art enthusiasts and curious visitors alike. Soft, golden lights illuminated the grand hall, casting elegant shadows upon the polished wooden floors and cream-colored walls, which were adorned with exquisite paintings. At the entrance, an intricately designed label gracefully welcomed the guests:

'Chilanka: The Timeless Chimes of Womanhood – An Exhibition of Paintings by Artist Charulatha Chittezham' (*Chilanka*, in *Malayalam*, denotes delicate ankle bells, echoing feminine grace and rhythm.)

Charulatha, dressed elegantly in a flowing black attire, stood motionless, lost in contemplation before one of her most striking portraits. Her eyes lingered thoughtfully upon two watchful faces depicted behind wooden attic louvres, their gazes intense yet mysteriously concealed.

A short distance away, her mobile phone vibrated persistently on a polished teak table, its screen lighting up intermittently. The day had indeed been demanding, bustling with interactions and accolades, yet it marked one of the most fulfilling chapters of her artistic journey.

'I've grown more patient,' Charu silently acknowledged, letting out a gentle sigh of relief as the gallery gradually emptied, leaving her alone amidst the quiet embrace of her creations.

It took months to accomplish her long-held aspiration of hosting a solo exhibition of her creative art. She did, a few times at the University College and could open marquees in association with the kindred spirits.

Charu hadn't taken her artistic fervor seriously until she experienced its therapeutic effects. Initially, it served as a deliberate distraction, but recently it has become her savior. The apprehensions that held her back for so long gradually faded, giving way to feelings of self-esteem and acceptance.

The hour clock didn't seem to be moving. She had been waiting to see Kodi since last October and was never allowed to make calls to her. They had fewer conversations after the night of Kodi's eventful description. It was harrowing for Charu to think of Kodi's plight, who had to keep herself away from her daughter and grieve in seclusion.

That day, too, was one of waiting. Kodi had promised to show up online two weeks back. But the call didn't come. To Charu, the period of abeyance became one for creation.

She decanted her imagination about how Kodi, as a woman, would be on canvas. She was eager to show it to Kodi.

Charu became so outstretched by the bustling activities in the hall that she could hardly attend to any calls. After hours, she noticed a video call from an unfamiliar number.

It was a dark, lean woman on the other side. Her eyes smiled more than her lips could offer. But there was no light in them.

"Kodi"

Charu stood aghast.

Kodi looked quite contrary to Charu's expectations, all shattered. Prolonged torment and suffering had lined and damaged her face. Charu struggled with her emotions after seeing a long-lost playmate in a disheartening way.

"Kodi, see how she looks. I tried to paint you. But it's a lot different!"

Charu deliberately wanted to ease her shock a little bit by displaying Kodi's portrait to her.

"Charu..."

Kodi laughed until she let out a cry and suddenly hung up the phone. But her voice said everything: the pain of a helpless woman, the uncertainty in waiting, a woman who felt forsaken by hope.

After that, Charu frequently spoke to Kodi, her sole aim being to console her. She gradually became a strong shoulder for the distressed woman, whom health issues frequented quite often. Kodi's diagnosis had been made late in 2021. She had been given pre-ART counseling, and the initiation of the antiretroviral therapy (ART) gave her hope. Kodi's insecure feelings gradually got unwound.

'The government provides for us. I get my treatment in Chennai.'

She didn't want Charu to spend money on her, and she never wanted to let Charu be with her.

Her daughter, Amutha, was a graduate student. Unfortunately, the girl had lost a few academic years. Kodi never wanted to compromise on her daughter's education and did all she could to make her independent. Much to her relief, Kodi's sisters began visiting her.

"If at all something happens to me, there should be someone to take care of my Amutha. Doctors say that regular medication keeps us sustained. And I feel I have so much to do the rest of my time. A lot of people suffer like me; women and children are afflicted for no fault of their own. We are untouchable to others."

"But, Kodi, you are not to me. It's you who doesn't allow me to come to you. Why? And I am not like the others." Charu interrupted.

“I feel at home talking to you this way. Maybe someday we will meet.”

Kodi had no clear answer for that. But it seemed she had been in the grip of anxiety.

Charu turned to unwrap something.

“I have preserved you here with me, Kodi...”

She brought her phone in front of a picture of two girls standing inside an attic. In the background were a bamboo basket full of toys, an empty winnowing sieve, a clay jar, a torn mat, and a spittoon.

“Oh, girl. How beautifully you have recreated them!”

Kodi gave a wide smile.

“Whoever left me lives with me. I keep them somehow, like Achamma. She still resides in the betel box. I am happy that you have your relations. It’s a great feeling. I know because I lost all—my blood. Can we ever be back to our *machchu*, yes, right?”

Kodi was taken aback by what Charu said.

“What happened? Did you hear me?”

Charu noticed a change in Kodi’s expression.

“Things are not what they seem, Charu. Don’t you know anything?”

“What?”

"What I heard that day. I can still remember it as if it happened yesterday."

Kodi became contemplative.

"Why do you beat about the bush, Kodi?"

Charu got agitated.

"Do you remember that day when that man with a *turban* came home?"

"Yes, I do. Ambika Ammayi's husband. After Achamma's death."

Charu nodded pensively.

"What about Ambika Ammayi, Charu? You didn't mention her during our calls!"

The woman's name struck Charu suddenly.

"She always despised me. I don't know why. She was so different among the four. It was she who pushed me to that marriage and kept blaming me for its failure. How would I be responsible for someone's strange and irresolvable nature? You know, she wanted me to cling to that relationship and wanted to grab all my father's property. But her greedy plans didn't work. Good riddance! She expired some ten years back. I have no contact with her family in Punjab. I don't enquire after anybody other than you. I am Unnikrishnan's daughter; my father had never been hateful towards anybody. So am I."

Charu resumed sceptically.

"But, Kodi, why would you linger there now?"

"Because you mentioned *muchchu* today. You showed it to me. I have been thinking about whether to tell you that or not since I found you. Charu, you don't belong there."

Kodi's voice was feeble as she paused.

"You mean the *machchu*? You are right. It has been years since I left it. But it's still fresh in me. Shall we..."

"Charu, it's not that. Listen to me. Maybe what I am going to tell you might be inconceivable for you. It might break you."

Kodi continued interruptingly,

"I was up alone in the attic. You were downstairs. And I overheard them saying something about you that day."

"About me! Who said what?"

Charu creased in confusion.

"Ambika Ammayi and your father. There was Ammoppol too. They were forcing your father to marry. And Ambika Ammayi said..."

Charu leaned closer, listening to her agog.

Kodi's memory drew thirty-five years back to Chittezham. The whole conversation came alive in front of her once again.

❖ ❖ ❖

Ambika was sitting with Unnikrishnan. Her husband had a fondness for silence, and he kept looking at her throughout her talk.

"Why do you spoil your life like this, Unni? You are getting older. The dead one will never be back to you. Losing a life in the name of emotions is foolishness. You should think of marrying someone. And one more thing. Charu is not yours. Mind it. No one is there to tell you all this. I am the only blood relation you have. Here, nobody, not even Amma, can convince you of these. I am so sad for you, Unni."

Ambika kept reproving Unnikrishnan.

"How could you look down on my emotions? It's mine. You will never understand. And what did we have, Chechi? If Amma had not been merciful, where else would we have gone? What were we? We do exist simply because of her."

Sadness clung to Unnikrishnan's throat as he spoke.

"You are right. But Amma shouldn't have burdened you with her obsession. That's not right, Unni. You are never what she wanted. When are you going to realise that you are just a substitute?"

The woman's strain was evident on her face.

"Chechi, please stop saying that. It's I who did her death rites as her son. She used to tell me that I should do everything for her. Both Ammoppol and Kochoppol have stood by me. They never take us as outcasts. Your present happiness is the outcome of Amma's effort. We should not forget our roots, Chechi. It's she who married you off. Today is the last day of her final rites. Are you here to hurt her soul? Let her leave from here peacefully."

The woman leaned towards Unnikrishnan and said,

"Unni, I am not denying what you said. What I am saying is, (paused for a while) ...leave the girl, Charulatha is not our blood. Have your own life. You are a man."

"Chechi, hush, Charu might hear," Unnikrishnan said worriedly.

It was then Ammoppol entered there, with her remark.

"Time is flying, Unni. To have a partner for life is important. We will take care of her. Won't you be here for a few days, Ambika?"

There was no further discussion after that.

❖ ❖ ❖

Kodi halted and slid a serene look at Charu.

"Finished? Kodi, I love stories. But that doesn't mean you can say whatever you want to entertain me. Stop lying. Do you realize the seriousness of this situation? You're saying that I'm not of that blood and that even my father didn't belong there. How outrageous these allegations are! I can't take that. Do you understand? I don't have time for this nonsense. Good night!"

It was an unfamiliar face that Charu showed up in response to Kodi.

"Charu, stay there. Why should I lie to you? I have no reason to mislead you. I am a hopeless woman. I have no gains here. I tried to tell you about this, many times then. I wanted to reveal this even on the day I left Chittezham. However, I was sad and had feelings of uncertainty as a child. Truly, I have no further ideas related to you. But I cannot forget what I heard there. Charu, no matter how hard you try to refuse it, the truth will be the same. I don't want to see you sad. But..."

Charu's palpitating fingers aimlessly traversed through the canvas. Among the two girls, the little one's gaze locked with Charu's.

❖ ❖ ❖

CHAPTER 17

MADIRASIPPETTI – THE LOOP OF LIES

The loop. The loop, you know, that of lies, had enamoured me until that moment. I wanted to untangle it. I would instead flow like my river than stay stagnant because I didn't know how to remove the scaly scums that lay layered in multitude over me. But I wanted to. I longed to breathe in my own identity whatsoever. That's what made me dig deep.

I had to go far beyond Lachu Akka's words, embracing the meanness in me. That journey of mine opened up windows to the secrets in some lives. I could eavesdrop on their conversations as if I were watching them. As I mentioned, some stories are revealed on their own. Agavan and Kodi were the driveways to them. I would never have known myself, had there been no second meeting with Kodi, perhaps. The rest was my part.

I was dubious about the verity of Kodi's words. Even if I yelled at her, I trusted her strongly. Her words boomed in my head. The whole night, my thoughts drifted back to my childhood. Why would Achan mention 'outcasts'? What made Ammayi say that Achan was a substitute? Why didn't they tell me anything? Somebody, at least Kochoppol could have. She was the last one to leave.

I questioned their shadows and spoke to their remains. I performed many counts in the past when they were alive. But never did I receive responses. I said sorry to Lachu Akka. For, none could I wait for the invasion. I removed the latches and broke into the closed chambers on my own. I remembered having one such search that got me to Kodi's address.

I thanked myself for bringing at least some Chittezham keepsakes with me. The smell of incense effuses from Achamma's wooden chest each time I open it to get the betel box out. I never keep it empty. Years elapsed. Yet, the radiant peacock feather, kept inside her *Bhagavatham*, has not paled.

The only thing I hadn't approached was Ammoppol's iron trunk box, which was kept inside Achan's bedroom. That night, I unlocked it. The flakes of green paint stuck to my fingers, revealing the rust beneath.

As I opened it, the trunk grunted and wailed like a wounded animal. I expected to find some of Ammoppol's garments and utensils inside, as she always adored being dressed up well and had a special fondness for stainless steel articles. However, the box resembled a deep, rectangular unit of a mobile bookstore. 'Ammoppol was not a woman of letters!' I wondered.

There was a heavy silver cup on which engraved the letter R. An old wooden pen holder with calendar slides lay toppled over the massive dusty diaries. Even though my impatience grew to get all the chattels out, I gave utmost care not to damage any of them. They were like the stillborns in my arms, all silent. But all had eyes open to their worlds.

A few yellowed dailies in English and Tamil lay crumbled amidst those diaries. There were albums and photographs bearing the residues of years. Those I had seen inside Ammoppol's secret chamber, and some unfamiliar ones, too, were there. One was her staff photo taken in 1989. It showed Rajiv Gandhi, the then Prime Minister of India. I recognised another photograph with everyone at Chittezham except me.

One particular frame with Ammoppol and a little boy was missing among them. However, later I found it alongside the heaviest diary, dated back to 1947. They had been kept in the side compartment, the tilted edge of which was rusted. A few files were stacked inside, along with a collection of inland letters and postcards. It was difficult to remove them. I made it.

I carefully rummaged through the bottom of the trunk. Its depth was cluttered with solid objects. Some diaries lay bound together with lace there. A toy police car and a doll brought me smiles in those late hours of the night.

The doll wore a red satin frock with a fancy pouch attached to it. My smile vanished as I saw her face. It was a one-eyed doll. The only eye that remained open was blue. The last thing I got from the box was a tatty, worn-out silk sari wrapped in plastic. Along lay some pieces of clay dolls. From their tainted colours and shapes, I realised they were the *Thanjavur bobblehead dolls*. They remained crushed under the weight. 'Why had she left the brittle ones under? Perhaps they took a tumble inside the box.' I speculated.

My significant hope was to get a locket from the trunk mentioned by Kochoppol. She said such a thing belonged to me and had been with Ammoppol, but I didn't find anything similar to a locket.

I wished Kodi's words were just stories from somebody else's life. I placed the photographs on the cot and the toys on the adjacent mahogany table. Diaries were inside Ammoppol's Madras apartment, too, but I had never seen her carrying even a single one at Chittezham. Of course, she had the habit of reading magazines and newspapers, but she had never been a bibliophile!

I skimmed through her diaries. She had skipped dates in so many pages and had left pages unwritten. They were more like notebooks in which she had scribbled mainly in Malayalam and English. Words in them looked like rows of black ants.

'Everybody has secrets. I, too, have some. Charulatha is not someone well-known to others. I have another face.' I looked in the mirror, reflecting on myself. 'Maybe Ammoppol's diaries wanted to say something.'

I began with the one that was found in the side chamber first. By year, it was the oldest among all the diaries I got from the box. The year 1947 heightened my interest. The initial pages were blank. I was curious to see if there was something in the August pages, particularly on August 15th. And there was...

❖ ❖ ❖

15 August 1947

Dear Diary,

This is a new beginning for all of us. Our soil got freedom finally. Our jubilation knows no bounds. Amma's laughter makes me even happier. You know well how unsteady she has been since Unni passed away. I am happy today seeing both moms smiling. As I hoped, Unni has brought prosperity to us. May it remain longer! It doubles my joy and peace to tell you that I am boarding for Coimbatore soon, for my studies. Uncle is taking me there. I will certainly take you there.

Ammu

❖ ❖ ❖

I got confused about who were the two mentioned there! I took the first page where she had thanked her uncle for gifting that diary. I turned further. She had jotted down happy moments only. Amidst them, I noticed one detailed entry in which I read a tale. A true tale.

❖ ❖ ❖

10 May 1947

Dear Diary,

Things continue to amaze us. I have been fed up with the stories that haunt us viciously. But this one is not a fairy tale. It happened five days back. We went to the Viruthi temple festival.

You know, how Amma loves Kathakali! But she is not willing to go anywhere. Her last visit to the temple was three years ago, when someone played a joke on her, claiming that Lord Shiva had manifested inside the Sanctum Sanctorum. I still remember how she ran out of the house that day in tears. She just grabbed her Kachamundu off the clothesline, wound it on her chest, and darted towards the temple. I laughed at her on her return. She said she wanted to meet Him to seek a way to remove her family's curse forever. I couldn't say a word back to her innocent faith.

She hasn't left the house since then. She always squats down, casting a smile upward. And we often see her near the breadfruit tree. She talks to it for hours. Sometimes, she laments to my father, calling him, while asleep. Our hearts break. But what's the point of crying? I am not supposed to. Poor Kochu! She is scared to stay with her. Amma was not like this earlier. People still visit her to remove the evil eye from their children. However, they are unaware of how distressed she becomes each day. Ammavan has assured me to take her to the doctor of mind.

So, I just wanted to give Amma a distraction from all. We came home late after the Prahlada Charitham - Kathakali at the temple. The night was sweltering. After reaching home, Amma continued to complain about the noise coming from the old barn. We were shocked to see something distressing there.

The woman who used to bring a small flock of goats here was lying in a pool of blood. There was a baby boy by her side. She died after delivering it. It was Amma who cut the umbilical cord. We heard his first cries. Amma laughed and cried hilariously at the same time. She held the baby and ran to the Kalikavu to say prayers. She moaned, calling Devi and Naga deities.

"Oh, Devi...May this child stay with us! He is not of our blood. Don't take him away. I plead to you in the name of all my good deeds in all my lives so far."

I cannot describe the agony in Amma's words that night. The small girl, probably her daughter, whom we had met with the woman, was sitting near the door in tears. They seemed to have reached Chittezham by night. We don't know who the woman was and where she was from. But they came here twice, a few months back. Amma gave them full meals too. But she had told the woman that her goats could not be brought into our premises. I am not sure if that woman understood any of Amma's words. She was dumb and just nodded to Amma's questions and gestures. And I remember how Amma strained to hold back her tears while serving the pregnant woman and her daughter.

The little boy has brought a drastic change in Amma's nature. She never keeps him down. She says that he is our Unnikrishnan's rebirth and that he will bring new sunshine to our land. Anyway, we feel happy. We call him our Unni. Our little brother. The girl is younger than Kochu. Where would she go? Amma says we will keep her too. She gave her name too—Ambika - synonym of goddess.

But, I am worried. What if someone comes claiming the boy? Amma cannot stand that. So I, too, wish. May no one come for him!

Ammu

❖ ❖ ❖

There was nothing I desired from Ammoppol's trunk except for a locket. Yet, it started revealing its secrets. The story unsettled me. Kodi was indeed correct, as was Ambika Ammayi. Achan does not belong to Chittezham. I pored over the entry repeatedly and verified the dates to ensure my perception was accurate. I realized my father was a far more captivating storyteller than Ammoppol. He ensnared me with riddles and concealed puzzles as if they were a maze.

❖ ❖ ❖

CHAPTER 18

THE BURIAL OF LOVE – AN AUTUMN TALE

Despite the heat of that March, I felt as though I was frozen. A sea was around me—a dark one that tossed me to drown in its amorphous depths of qualms. Nothing could well recount the state of my mind that night. I felt like sitting on my heart, and it began imploding. Chittezham had never frightened me with the stories of its dark corridors. For the first time in my life, the house overhung me like a monster on a huge canvas.

The trunk remained open, but I lacked the courage to reexamine the objects. I didn't want to spend my evening hours at home. I needed an escape. But from what? Little Charu smiled at me like the one-eyed doll in front of me. My paintings, the women in my life that I exhibited, began laughing at me.

For me, the unknowns in the box were substantive. They were the only speakers of truth; the shadows that could show me the path to myself. No matter how hard I tried to escape them, they kept reminding me of the confounding reality. I had to resume reading them. And I did. It was not simply a carrier. It was more than that—the fact I confirmed so soon. I spent days and nights reading those annals or simply dumping myself before them.

I saw sullen faces—their hopelessness. The desperate situations that Achamma had confronted in her youth came flooding back to me. I had heard about some from her in my childhood. But they appeared to me like the half-moon-shaped orange candies. I used to enjoy them, expecting them always to be sweet. But they tasted bitter inside. Everybody at Chittezham was like the toffee cover doll that Achan had taught me to make. They were just images far removed from the real ones.

I learned that somebody called Subhadra had been endeared to Achamma. The night of the deluge, the attic, the toddler's death, and the blind grandmother. How time snatched each one from Achamma! Everybody except two girls. I felt them, flesh and blood, in those tainted pages.

The pain of women and mothers and their cries of a century fell into my ears. The ancient story that everyone believed to be true about *Kalikavu* was not a myth. The pages proved it. Lives proved it. Ammoppol had recorded everything there as she could. The curse was on men. But the disastrous consequences were borne by the females, crushing them to pieces all while alive.

Yes. Ammoppol's diary was telling me true tales.

Unnikrishnan was Parvathy's hope. She never laid him down. Days and nights, she guarded him and fed him with her tender love. The doleful woman's passivity gradually changed.

Ammoppol was never frail. We had seen her as a self-made woman of strong willpower. I considered her a ruler who held kingdoms in her possession. Most of the time, I perceived her as a haughty despot. She was the decision-maker at Chittezham, and her words were final in every situation. Her unfeeling approach stood in stark contrast to everything around her.

She had been diligent in executing her official duties. I have often wondered how someone without gentle feelings could thrive in such a profession. But... but the blue diary, the smallest of all, of C. Rajalakshmi proved to be iconoclastic. I barely knew the woman in it. It shattered all my impressions of Ammoppol, whom I thought I had known at Chittezham.

In the diary, she began by apologizing for her absence from the habit of documenting events for a few years. Within those pages, I felt I was with a girl named Rajalakshmi. Her youthful exuberance created captivating rambles in those entries, reflecting a time when she was new to her practical service at the Madurai Medical College Hospital.

'He often teased me by calling me an angry Angel with a bindi. I didn't like that in the beginning. But... It all began on that Christmas Eve.'

That's how Ammoppol starts narrating her secret story.

'We never celebrate at Chittezham. Though I want to give them moments of happiness, that's all... I just wish Amma, Kochu, Ambika and Unni... to be peaceful and safe. The invisible threat is always there. And most of the time, it suffocates me. The stress I try to bury in me often hinders my work. I wish Achan were there. He might not return. Amma still keeps waiting. But I have lost hope. And I won't let anything happen to them.

Things are so different here in Madurai. I love being here, among these staff and student nurses like me. I forget everything that upsets me. I see people who celebrate life here, even in scarcity. They are so carefree. Sometimes, I am unable to be one among them, but they bring me joy and fun. When will I be like them?'

I felt Ammoppol in front of me, confiding in me all her frustrations and secrets.

That's when I learned about how she fell in love with a junior doctor at an early stage in her career. She feared falling in love. But it happened. It was a time when female nursing staff were restricted from entering marital relations. For Rajalakshmi, her career was something indispensable to her family's livelihood. Still, it happened. Nowhere in the diary did she mention his name. But each word brimmed with her love for that man. They met on the eve of the celebration when she acted out the role of an angel.

'Angels don't stick bindi...'

He laughed at her calling *'Angel with bindi.'* The young man was from Thanjavur. I accompanied both lovers in the hospital rooms, temples, and cities. Their expeditions had been countless, but only a few were chronicled in those pages.

He once took her to Thanjavur to meet his family. He was the only son of his parents. Ammoppol kept the matter a secret at Chittezham. Besides, somewhere in her mind, she was pulled down from the idea of disclosing to him about her family curse.

There were blank pages in between. She continued the events after a huge intermission.

'I didn't want to lose him. I loved him that much. I never had the habit of praying. But love made me weaker, and I began pleading to the gods and goddesses to save my love and our relationship forever.

He frequently asked me for permission to come home and seek my hand in marriage. But I objected. I wanted him to wait. I delayed everything out of fear. But even before that, our love had been consumed. I became pregnant. His assurances seemed to me stronger than the power of any curse on earth. And I accepted him as my husband at the Madurai Meenakshi Temple. Nobody witnessed our marriage save the goddess. I prayed my heart out for the good fortune of our unborn child and to protect my husband's lineage. His parents, who had been willing to join our union, got displeased with our love ventures.

Dear Diary,

All those years I couldn't write you. Just like I kept myself away from Chittezham for a longer period, I put you aside. I wrote letters to Amma but kept them unsent. It was my secret. And I wanted to protect it, unharmed by any of the elements of Chittezham. My focus had been wavering. I felt under threat. I prayed for a baby girl. But...

Our Sri Kumaran was born as a healthy boy. My husband's parents were happier to receive the news, and those days were my best as a newborn mom. I often took him to the temples and prayed for my son's longevity.

It was the last phase of autumn when our Sri succumbed to ascites. Although we were in the medical field, we couldn't save him. He fell as a leaf. A mere leaf. I used to dream how my mother would carry my boy in her arms with full laughter and that, one day, his footsteps would garland the soil of Chittezham. And I dream that every moment. Even now...

Did I want to fail all the belief systems over my family and soil? I don't know. But I failed in front of the mysterious plot of destiny. I realised. The curse would never spare our blood. Wherever we run, it would catch us and leech us dry.

It was that day that I could relate to my mother's pain. I wanted to save my husband. I could not think of him suffering because of our ominous fate. I forced him to leave me. I asked for forgiveness from his parents for my failure to give a baby in their family line. I convinced them of the gravity of the situation

I have been in. All I did was because I loved him, my love more than my life.

Once he stood obstinately by me, I had no other way than to force myself to leave him forever. What's left with me are those Thanjavur dolls, the lover-couple he had gifted to me before our marriage. And the Kancheepuram silk sari that I wore on the day of our marriage.

I returned to Chittezham after a two-year absence. 'Those years were my nursing practical period.' I had already given Amma such a notion. It was true in a way. Unni turned ten that year. I was weak and fell into his little arms. I felt my brother, no, my son, holding me tightly, not letting me fall. There was a wailing, violent storm within. But it was never meant to lament. I held back its murmurs and began shrinking into my silence.

I didn't give Amma a face for days, fearing I would break myself. I could sometimes hear her footsteps near the door, but she hasn't asked me anything until now. I often doubted if she had any clue about my situation.

I had to pursue my course, which had been incomplete, in Madurai. I didn't find my husband there. He had already moved somewhere far away. The thought of him pestered me. After a while, we met at a medical conference in Madras. By then, he had been married. I spoke to him one last time. I asked him not to curse me for having broken him. His eyes were wet then. I knew I could not claim him back. I didn't want to. But, to tell you the truth, often I don't have the strength to accept reality.

Still, I struggle... Will we meet again? I know life will be like the clay dolls and the moth-eaten silk sari. It is so fragile!'

The image of an arrogant woman collapsed in front of me, giving way to an unselfish soul. My heart wept with Ammoppol. I could live those moments with her, touch her pain. What she penned was shocking. They were not Rajalakshmi's confessions. Rather, they showed me someone who tried to fight destiny yet stooped before the unseen forces. The world saw her as a spinster, but she wasn't one.

I have heard and known many love stories. And how the one that I am involved in has wrung me. Ammoppol's diary records shook me to the realization that shades of love are possible anywhere and anytime, and some grievances remain for a lifetime. Sometimes the scars leave you aggrieved or occasionally complacent. It might make you an alien, miserably strolling on the charred chasms of some dry land. Hopes didn't rain on her soil. She might have resented it, therefore. And just stayed on.

Ammoppol completed her studies and entered her career. She became a certified midwife and ideal in her service as a nursing tutor. She was the breadwinner of her family. The young lady ascended to be powerful and headstrong. Chittezham prospered. Achamma considered it a miracle. She believed that it was all brought by Achan.

❖ ❖ ❖

CHAPTER 19

THE CASKET OF WHISPERS

The dawn had already entered the room. My eyes caught sight of Ammoppol and her son. A chink of daylight glared at them. I had never seen even a slit of a smile from Ammoppol. But there she stood with one in the frame before me.

How would her heart have ached? A mother's? My fingers grazed over the two.

'Amma remarkably transformed after Unni's birth. Even a momentary separation from him became miserable for her.'

Ammoppol continued giving me a riveting read. I could hardly wait for each day to end, to return to those folds. One of the narrated incidents, when Achan was in high school, brought me happy tears.

'Whenever Amma grated coconut, he demanded a mouthful of it. And she would chide the naughty boy, playfully. Unni would then play pranks on her by loudly reciting the lines from Vyloppilli Sreedhara Menon's poem Mambazham, which would make Amma cry, and she would soon feed him the whole of it

by hand. At those times, all I could do was shut myself up. I am even deprived of the right to tears.'

I could imagine how those lines could have stirred the deep-seated disturbances in a mother's heart. I discovered them between the lines.

'Unni and Ambika would be safe. But Kochu! Concern about her grows on me. I don't want the same misfortune to fall upon my innocent sister. I am unable to convince anybody of my concrete reason to desist from marriage. But Amma seems to understand me better. She is worried about Kochu and has started seeking proposals for her.'

People hesitated to have an alliance with Chittezham. But the parents of Plakkoottil Kesavan Nair wanted Kochoppol as their son's bride. They thought marriage would assuage his wanton ways. Kochoppol didn't have a choice, either. She feared being a burden to others. Nobody was there to enquire about the bridegroom, and the marriage was fixed in the absence of Ammoppol. For the first time, Ammoppol raised against her uncle, culminating in a total uproar in the family.

'Ammu, if you don't want to be married, stay away. Let her.'

It was Achamma who intervened.

'Here comes a big money maker! Such arrogance! This is what happens if girls are educated. She doesn't even know how to talk to elders. It's my fault. Do you people value any of my words? Is this an inn to accommodate wanderers?...'

The last of Krishnan Nair's words angered Achamma, and she asked him to stop.

'You and your waywardness! Don't call me for anything.'

With that, Krishnan Nair stopped visiting Chittezham. Even if Achamma tried to placate her brother so many times, he didn't heed.

'Why would my words irritate him? After all, I have a responsibility, too. Kochu is my blood. She has skills and a great interest in Malayalam Literature. She writes poems, too. Her soft-spoken and obedient nature doesn't mean she should suffer because of others' imprudence.'

Ammoppol wondered.

She was right. That union was never an appropriate decision. Kesavan Nair didn't change much after the marriage and became even worse. Ammoppol tried maximum to save Kochoppol's pregnancies. But all ended up in abortion before the second trimester. Therefore, in a way, each time, she was saved from having the plight to bear the pain of loss after a full-term pregnancy.

I passed through each book there one after the other.

All at Chittezham rejoiced at Ambika Ammayi's wedding. My father accompanied Ambika Ammayi's husband to many places, where he could try different jobs. It was in his early twenties he visited Calcutta.

'Unni mentions some Jyothi, a girl from Alappuzha who is settled in Calcutta with her parents. He reports everything to me. He says he wouldn't have met her if he hadn't gone to Calcutta. How happy he blooms at the mention of her name! As he says, maybe, she is meant for him. He wants to marry her. But it's a bit early now. We tell him to wait for a few more years. Besides, the girl's parents must also come to terms. I have told him my wish to meet her in person. Anyway, the girl is lucky if she gets our Unni. He is such a caring boy.'

Their relationship grew to the point where they couldn't bear to be apart. Ammoppol planned to visit the girl's ancestral home during that year's *Onam*.

I soon found many pages blank and her notes continued in the penultimate pages of that diary.

'I had to go and bring him back home. He hasn't spoken a word since the accident. We cannot stand seeing him being in the throes of this worst phase. How long will it take to heal him from the pain? Who might better understand the pain of losing someone? We didn't meet Jyothi. Still, she was like our family. And this loss, we cannot shrug off. I was wrong. She is not in his destiny... Unni is our sunshine. But this gloom overshadows everything.'

The girl whom my father had loved died in a train crash in Bombay, in 1978. The changes in my father were apparent in Ammoppol's description. The usual agility in him left him ultimately.

'Amma fears to leave him alone these days. Even I feel he might end up destroying himself. I cannot bear to see him this way. I am taking him to Madras. He needs a break from all.'

Even if Ammoppol took him to Madras, he was hardly able to recover to normal. Ambika Ammayi wanted to take him with her. But he remained hesitant throughout.

'Today, he broke down. He cried on Amma's lap. I had seen him weeping this way on that day when Amma revealed everything to him about his birth. It was her own decision to reveal and she made it before Ambika's marriage. Even though she had a fear of losing him, she felt it was required for the safe marriage of Ambika. And, luckily, she didn't fail. Unni rather grew too emotional and began adoring Amma. Sometimes I feel Amma is the only reason why Unni is still alive. Her affection and care do help in bringing him back to normal.'

I recollected my father telling me the story of the nymph. Was he crying then? Yes. I saw his lashes wet. And it took years for me to know all of these. My heart beat faster as my eyes traversed those diaries in front of me. I couldn't wait to find one. 'Whom did he marry then? What if I am not my father's child?'

There were no diaries left in the box. I looked into it again and again and realised I was standing at a dead end. I needed to ask someone. And I kept asking each of their shadows. There were some letters and postcards left. I saw letters from Kochoppol and Achan. And some were written in Tamil which I couldn't read. I should have kept my word to Lachu Akka by learning the language.

I sobbed calling out for them. I held them closer to my forehead.

My father's room bore the semblance of a museum. And the trunk was much like a burial urn kept inside. I was reminded of my visits to the Napier Museum with Achan. He had answers to all my queries there. He made me read the description under each artefact and added something from his take on them.

It's well-lit. Somewhere familiar. I could see my father smiling at me. I started calling him. But he was not paying heed. I felt lost.

"Charu..."

Unnikrishnan was searching for Charu. He lost the girl in one of the corridors of Napier Museum and kept calling her.

"Where am I? Achaa... (in a tone of calling)"

Charu screamed. She panted until he came near her. She hugged him tightly. The girl had a similar experience once at *Thekkinkadu Maidanam* (also known as *Thekkinkadu Ground*) during their visit to attend the *Thrissur Pooram.* (a *Hindu* temple festival in Thrissivaperur, celebrated annually in the Malayalam month of *Medam*). After that event, she was too afraid to join the crowd. But this time too...

"Don't leave me, Achaa..."

Charu sulked and wept. Unnikrishnan tried to cheer her up by showing the exhibits. They walked on and on...

"Do you know what this one is, daughter?"

Charu looked at the object and shook her head.

"This is called the Burial Urn. It's a kind of coffin. Some used to keep the corpse in such vessels. See the description down."

The girl was amazed.

"But why so?"

"Perhaps they didn't have space to contain their struggles."

Charu stood a bit bewildered.

"Didn't you understand? I said they didn't have space outside. Therefore they went inside."

Unnikrishnan's laughter came as an appendage before Charu could ask anything again.

The girl, too, giggled. But her eyes were searching for the corpse. It was dark inside. The vessel suddenly took the shape of a trunk.

"Charu... Charu..."

I found myself smiling as I woke up. My tears had wet those diaries. I just fell asleep while holding them. But I met my father many years later. The dream ended before I could ask him anything. I thank those dreams that bring me the lost ones. Yes, dreams bring them, too.

The corpse! My eyes plunged into the dark nooks of the box. It didn't appear to contain anything. Still, I felt like looking further. In the torchlight, I could see something inside the side chamber—that rust. My arm bled as I groped inside. They had been crammed and stuck there. I felt the ones inside lighter and struggled to get them out. I finally retrieved one booklet and a mini diary. I was breathless as I opened them. I leafed through them, hoping to read my name. But I didn't find it anywhere. The diary was addressed to someone else —a stranger. It read:

To Vaigai, our baby doll...

❖ ❖ ❖

CHAPTER 20

LETTER TO VAIGAI

The scorched earth sighed softly, haunted by memories of last year's rains. The sky, barren and indifferent, withheld its compassion, leaving the earth yearning to soothe the tiny tongues still sleeping deep within her womb.

In Usilampatti, the culverts lay dormant, silently enduring the relentless monotony of the drying soil. They appeared like weary eyes gazing blankly into lives cloaked in shadow. The summer sun had baked these channels into lifeless veins, resembling ashtrays filled with dull, crumbling earth. Their winding paths narrowed toward alleyways that led into the clustered palm-thatched huts of the village Vembatti.

Sparse trees stood scattered across the parched stubble fields that stretched alongside the canals. Clusters of delicate white and pale purple flowers intermingled with bold oleander blooms, their faces peering curiously over the edges. A dry breeze swept past, rustling through the foliage, competing with the cacophony of restless cattle grazing in the distance.

Seven-year-old Kokila hurriedly lifted the tiny puppy from the ditch near the abandoned well and dashed toward home. It had been whimpering helplessly since the previous night, surrounded by swarming ants. With determined urgency, Kokila brushed away the insects, scarcely noticing their bites in her eagerness to introduce her newfound companion to her little sister.

"Oh, it's so tiny, Akka! Its eyes aren't even open yet! Is it a boy?"

It was Kala, Kokila's five-year-old sister, whose lively chatter filled the air.

"Hey girl... Why should you be bothered? Go and leave it back where you found it."

There came a command from an old woman who kept licking her cracked lips as she spoke. Dark lines etched into her weathered face imitated those dry furrows of the village. Like gnarled roots, delicate veins coursed up her neck, marking years of hardships and scarcity.

Kokila was hesitant to obey her paternal grandmother Nachiyamma. Both the sisters planned to keep the puppy home. But things were not to their expectation. Though they managed to keep the little one inside a carton, they couldn't ease its hunger. It was impossible to get some goat milk without their grandmother's permission.

"Amma, when will the baby come out? Won't you feed this pup after our baby's arrival ...?"

Kala smiled confidently at her mother Senbagam.

The pregnant Senbagam sat gazing at the wall in front of her. Her skin bore a dusky, livid hue. Both exhaustion and a lack of nourishment left her looking worn and fragile. Strands of coarse hair hung limply around her face, tangled and devoid of moisture. A small, sweat-stained yellow thread peeked out from her dull brown blouse. The other ornament she wore was a tiny neem stick, serving as a humble substitute for a traditional nosepin. It was apparent that she didn't want the hole to be cleared like her ear piercings.

Kala's chatter pulled her back from her thoughts. She had just returned from fetching water from a distant well located on the land owned by *Gounder* Sathyavel. (*Gounder* is a caste name.) All the nearby wells had run dry.

Like most other villagers, Nachiyamma and her husband Nallamuthu had worked on Sathyavel's farmland. Their sons, Thinakaran and Meyyan, also labored there. Senbagam had been brought into the marriage about eight years ago as Meyyan's bride from Usilampatti, and she, too, had started working as a housemaid at the *Gounder's* house.

The heat weighed heavily on her, amplifying her pregnancy fatigue, while the growing fear enervated her even more; a fear that expanded with her belly. Senbagam gasped uneasily and got up to unpack the food sent by Sathyavel's wife, Malliga.

Once she completed her seventh month, Senbagam had stopped going to the *Gounder's* house. The village was experiencing a tough time, marked by a significant decline in farming that year. Meyyan had not earned money for a while; he had just been hired to work at Sathyavel's foundry in Madurai recently.

By evening, Nallamuthu came on four feet. Arrack had subdued his senses. He puked a few times and fell onto the coir cot in front of the house. Kala was adamant about keeping the puppy by her for the whole night. The morning after, the girls didn't find the puppy inside the hut.

Getting irritated by its wails, Nallamuthu had already dragged it outside and buried it alive. Senbagam, too, was unaware of what had been done to the little creature. Kala went on crying until Senbagam took her to the *Gounder's* house. She wanted to get some old pieces of clothing from there. The two girls loved to go there, for the huge house had been a wonderful feast for both. They often got good food from there. *Gounder's* wife, Malliga, would occasionally send food to the girls through Senbagam.

The girl's sobs ceased as Malliga gifted her with an old doll that had once belonged to her eldest daughter, who had been married off. The doll was big for Kala and had beautiful blue eyes. It kept smiling at her. She had seen dolls in the neighbourhood, but not one as pretty as this. Kala was not ready to keep the dolly down, at least for a second. She bore it like a Kangaroo.

"Amma, is our baby like this?"

Senbagam became uncomfortable with that question.

"No. Not this time."

Meyyan muttered as he lit a *beedi* and passed a glance at Senbagam.

In the light flashed the man's thick sideburns stretched down to a droopy moustache. Behind them hid his firm and unsmiling lips.

"*Appa* ('father' in Tamil), why are all the dolls girls?"

Kokila's stare was all at her father's face when she raised that question.

Meyyan didn't say a word. He took a long puff and flicked the stub afar.

His coarseness always scared Kokila, and she didn't dare to enquire further.

The day after that, too, turned out to be a sad one for the girls. It so happened that the neighbourhood boy Kathir pierced a broomstick in the doll's eye on the pretext of a surgeon. The boy was notorious among the village children for his pranks.

Kokila and Kala tried shaking the doll to regain its lost eye, but it never came back. The girls' shrill screams drove their families crazy. Nachiyamma let her wilder spirits take over and struck up an argument with Kathir's grandfather,

Mariyappan. Thus, a child's pastime created a row in that alley.

It went on until Kathir's mother, Jaya, started writhing in labour pain. Her water broke and Nachiyamma was called in to attend the delivery. The old woman was a skilful midwife in Vembatti. It was she who delivered Kathir and two of his sisters.

The night guzzled the cries of Jaya's baby.

The following day, the heat was considerably high. Senbagam became even more exhausted that day and huddled inside the hut.

'Jaya has another daughter!'

Thoughts raced through her mind. She knew that her mother-in-law had gone along the field. She would either get the purple crown plant or the oleander. And that was normal once an unwanted girl was born into a family. Almost every house in and around the village locked the low wails of daughters destined to be departed that way.

Senbagam remembered Jaya's second baby, whom they used to call 'Venaponnu' (the unwanted girl). Such daughters had no names. It had been a custom to refer to them synonymously, to remind all that they were unwanted forever.

Venapponnu was born before Kathir. They didn't choose to give her the sour milk of the plant. But they weaned the infant early, which put it in hell. Like many other daughters around, she starved until she lost the battle. Jaya didn't cry when Venapponnu left. Nor was any mother supposed to.

'I wish I could have nipped her within before she was born! But how? I don't want it to suffer in the future. After all, they're a useless lot.'

Jaya's words were blunt. But that said it all. It was every mother's stance on that matter. No families ever mourned such dooms for their little girls. Instead, they were forced to anticipate wellness eventually. They had been accustomed to believing the weeds ought to be wiped out before welcoming the right crop.

Hurdles have been beyond measure for people raising children. Daughters, for them, had always been the bringers of losses and were least preferred, except those who were born as the first or second. They wouldn't earn from farms. And a lot must be spent on their marriage. Senbagam knew the hassles involved in the impoverished families in sending their girls into marriage.

'They are total damage to lives.'

In Usilampatti, Senbagam's parents often made that statement. She couldn't find any difference in Vembatti or any of the other villages nearby, either.

'You will have to do this. It is just a matter of a second, girl. And doesn't even take the time needed to defecate openly.'

Senbagam's eyes were almost vacant when Nachiyamma urged her to poison her third baby girl. It happened three years back when Kala was just two.

'It's not a sin, Senbagam. We cannot afford to have another. And I am sure that you will be blessed with a boy next time.'

Senbagam lay like a rock. The old woman didn't wait. She grabbed the baby off to a corner, dripped the milky sap into its tiny mouth, and prepared it to be set free for a world where no lullabies awaited.

Hours later, Senbagam screamed out, calling for the baby back. Nachiyamma consoled her by giving Kala in her arms. Thereafter, nightmares often visited her, and she held Kala and Kokila closer each time.

'Won't you be a boy? You have to be.'

Grief flooded out to drench Senbagam's fully grown bump, which she kept caressing. There was total silence within. No kicks had been there since midnight. She knew how her inner strife might have affected the little one.

Kokila and Kala were still asleep. Some footsteps came closer. Nachiyamma returned after the usual procedure. Her face was dull. She sat for a while on the upended container, staring numbly at Senbagam, and then left to bring water.

Time ticked away...

Hushed noises came out of Jaya's house. A little wobbly, with the weight of her belly, Senbagam peeped out through the crannied wall. A dark lean-bodied old man passed by, with a light wrap in his hands. It was Mariyappan, Jaya's father-in-law.

Earlier, the villagers preferred to bury the unwanted after nightfall. But over the years, the practice became so common that they began doing it at their convenience.

'Somewhere a baby girl would be born to be culled like that by someone!'

Senbagam cringed in sorrow. Her thighs began trembling. The girls were already awake. For hours that day, Nachiyamma didn't say a word to her daughter-in-law. The old woman could relate to the turmoil. Like many midwives and mothers, she had been committing gross actions for a long time.

'Senbagam, do not worry, girl. We will visit Meenakshi Koil as you wish. This time *Amman* (goddess) will definitely give us a boy. Look at your belly. I am sure it's one.'

Nachiyamma tried to console Senbagam, examining her lowered bump.

Since she got pregnant, Nachiyamma had been desperate to visit the Meenakshi temple with Senbagam. Every year in the summer season, during the month of *Chithirai* (Tamil month), she would visit her brother's house near Madurai. For now, she had special prayers to offer to goddess

Madurai Meenakshi to ask for a precious baby boy to be welcomed home. The woman wanted her daughter-in-law to be at the divine abode of *Meenakshi Amman* before her due date.

"What if it's not...?"

Senbagam stuttered.

"Senbagam, let it come out. We will see to the matter then."

"No. You will poison it, for sure. And I won't let you do that again."

Senbagam yelled.

Kokila and Kala came running home, listening to the shout-out.

"The nerve of this girl! Stop yelling here and give us a son, then. What do you think you would do? How will we bring them up? Do you think I am happy doing it?"

Nachiyamma became morbid, at last.

"I began this at the *Gounder's*, long back. Even the rich ones find it difficult to raise girls. Girls are like lit *beedi*, daughter. If not stubbed out in time, might go wild. All of us will get consumed. It happens with everyone here. What else can we do?"

There was silence after. Kala came crying and hugged her mother. Her one-eyed dolly got pressed down against Senbagam's bump.

Days went by...

The entrails of the earth were parched in the heat of April. The last of the drops, too, withered from the canals of Vembatti. *Vaigayar* (the River Vaigai) would be generous to them once she was full of the abundance from the western green hills. All waited for her little fingers, which were months away.

❖ ❖ ❖

CHAPTER 21

A RIVER NAMED SHADOW

The festival season had enveloped Madurai, draping the city in colors and sounds that persisted vibrantly for nearly a month. On this particular day, the city—usually alive with constant bustle—seemed overwhelmed, the streets swarming with an unprecedented throng of devotees. The air pulsated with rhythmic drumbeats, the resonant clang of cymbals, and the fervent chanting of thousands echoing through narrow lanes and broad avenues alike. *Chithirai Thiruvizha*, Madurai's grand annual Tamil Hindu festival centered at the majestic Meenakshi Temple, had drawn pilgrims from distant towns and villages, their faces aglow with devotion and excitement.

Richly ornamented chariots rolled slowly down crowded streets, glittering under the blazing sun, their surfaces adorned with intricate floral arrangements and shimmering fabrics that fluttered gently in the warm breeze. Each celestial vehicle carried deity idols dressed in luminous silks, their forms radiating divine majesty. Accompanying these sacred chariots surged a tide of devotees, their synchronized hymns and devotional songs rising in harmonious crescendo, vibrating with reverence and joy. Bunches of lush sugar cane tied with vibrant ribbons, baskets overflowing with freshly harvested grains, and assorted seasonal crops were meticulously arranged within elaborate pavilions, laid reverently as offerings to the divine.

Bordering the temple's northern perimeter flowed the River Vaigai, her waters glistening under the fading golden sunlight. Earlier that morning, she had felt the divine embrace of *Lord Kallazhagar*, revered as an incarnation of *Lord Vishnu*, whose idol, resplendent in vibrant green attire, had been ceremoniously immersed in her shallow, serene currents. Mounted atop his magnificent golden horse, the deity's presence had sanctified the waters, turning them into liquid blessings. As dusk approached, the Vaigai whispered gently, her ripples murmuring echoes of sacred chants, carrying divine hymns softly towards the twilight sky, mingling their melodies with the quiet rustle of leaves along her banks.

"This city never sleeps, Unni," Rajalakshmi uttered.

Unnikrishnan became captivated by the intricate carvings that proudly showcased the splendor of ancient Dravidian architecture. They had spent several days in the city, watching the festivities and rituals, with plans to depart for Viruthi the following week. An uninterrupted procession of bullock carts began to move slowly toward the outskirts, laden with people and supplies. The wooden cartwheels creaked intermittently, creating a rhythm that matched the hoofbeats...

"They are from remote villages. Many come with their offerings to the deities. And, you know, there are robbers too, among them."

"Robbers!"

Unnikrishnan stayed watchful.

A small girl waved at him in giggles from one of the carts. He waved back. Rajalakshmi's gaze was on the visibly pregnant woman with the girl inside.

'Oh! She is at full term. How can she be in a cart at this stage!' Rajalakshmi muttered.

A solemn silence enveloped the city as night fell. The moon flowed like a river above, illuminating the buildings with its radiant glow. The finials of the grand temple entrances created various patterns beautifully in the silver yards. The Vaigai resembled a slender white wick in an oil lamp, waiting for dawn to ignite it.

Some of Rajalakshmi's acquaintances had already departed from the city, but the siblings took a leisurely night walk, savoring the eclectic atmosphere around them. The street shops remained open, with a few carts still stationed in the northern area hedges.

Both retreated to a pavilion by the side of the river.

"Unni, you need to make a decision. Do not end up grieving. You have your future ahead. It's just a temporary job for you here. But you can find a better one and can continue here if you wish. Time doesn't wait for anything. Things change. They have to. Dear son, you must be positive about what I say. Change for your own sake. We will find you a bride."

"*Oppol*, please stop."

Unnikrishnan sat with a long gaze and heaved a sigh.

Memories took Rajalakshmi back to her youthful years.

"See the river. It has become thinner. You know, it was in 1959 that Vaigai Dam was inaugurated. Twenty-two years have passed. How fast time flies! I made my first visit here many years ago, during the early years of my career. My friends were with me then. I cannot forget those moments here. Those days and nights were the best I ever cherished. Tonight, it brings me pain. How blissful they were!"

She smiled and kept her eyes closed.

Shadows grew longer with each passing moment.

Somebody's muffled cries woke up Rajalakshmi from a trance.

"Isn't it a child crying, *Oppol*?."

Unnikrishnan anxiously searched in the dark. Rajalakshmi stepped down along the hedges. A woman lay there in labour pain. Standing beside her was a girl, crying.

She could identify both. It was the same woman whom she had seen in the cart a few hours back.

The woman couldn't be taken anywhere. Her baby was coming out.

"Unni, don't come here. Please take the girl with you. Let me help her."

Unnikrishnan took the girl up to the pavilion. She held a doll that had a single eye.

The night wore on with its rising lantern.

"*Penkolanthai, ma...*" (It's a baby girl.)

There was no response from the woman. Her gaze soon turned from the baby to the river that gleamed brighter in the white sun.

"Vaigai"

The woman whispered.

"What's your name? Tell me who is with you. Are you lost? I can help you."

Rajalakshmi's questions were not answered.

'Pasikkithu, Amma' (I am hungry.)

Unnikrishnan went southward in search of food. There was a solemn air on Rajalakshmi's face upon his return.

"What happened, Oppol? Did she say anything?"

Unnikrishnan stood in disbelief at what Rajalakshmi said about her situation.

The woman ate what he brought with great gusto.

The little girl was overjoyed at the sight of the baby near her mother. She was curious to give the doll to the newborn and started babying her.

“Let’s get you to your family.”

“No. I cannot take the baby to them. They will kill her. Save my Vaigai, Amma.”

The woman said plaintively.

Rajalakshmi realised the severity of the situation. She forcefully took them to the nearest health center. But by morning, there was no sign of her in the centre. She had already walked away in silence, leaving the baby there.

The city was crowded on consecutive days as well. They kept vigil over and searched thoroughly around for the woman for two more days. But she was nowhere to be found. Unnikrishnan intervened in Rajalakshmi’s plan to entrust the baby to some adoption center.

“These situations... How terrible they are! We are bait for them, mostly. Life is just a reminder of many losses and gains. We had losses. What if we accept this?”

“Unni, don’t be stupid. Philosophy won’t go in here. Be practical. You must not...”

Unnikrishnan didn't let her complete it.

"I know you also had losses, didn't you? Who else will know you better than me?"

All Rajalakshmi could do was stare at him in wonder.

"Let's own her, *Oppol*. Like you owned us. Like Amma did. Maybe this one is destined to be ours!"

There was no pause between what he spoke and did. Unnikrishnan hitched up his *mundu* and took the baby in his arms. He was trying to contain himself, then.

Rajalakshmi was amused to see the transformation in Unnikrishnan. A heartbroken youth soon turned out to be one with a clear conviction and a higher vision.

There was a locket around the baby's neck. The doll remained a silent witness, with its lone eye, unblinking.

❖ ❖ ❖

The night at the pavilion, your mother told me to save you from your people. Maybe, you had all in your family, including a father. Still, she wanted you to be away. Her description was short about how she had lost another girl before you and that there were many similar cases across. And she just vanished like that with the other girl. I did search for the woman who gave birth to you. I reported my experience to the authorities. But, people hushed up so much. They helped themselves from being trialled and tried.

The killing of baby girls had been a widely accepted practice in many villages there. People did it undercover using certain common methods. The harsher reality was that it was also known to many of the NGOs. Some had been complacent throughout. And such callousness carried a heavy price. Systems blinked for years, at times helplessly and at times evasively. They delayed endorsing the surreptitious act as a crime. I couldn't be blind to the situation, anyhow. And I tried to bring the attention of the masses to this. I wrote about it. This issue attracted considerable attention, with compelling articles, including mine, featured in newspapers. The gravity of the topic ignited its discussions and continued to fuel conversations in the decades to come.

People become fragile in the face of circumstances. Even if power comes with position, its enforcement is so uncertain. Many cases were reported in the following years too. An investigation into the matter was underway, which could lead to gradual changes. In the decades that followed, teams sprang into action, tirelessly visiting countless inner villages to spread awareness and inspire change. Of course things didn't change overnight. But, I am certain that there are a few daughters, like you, who have been saved in some way, in the years ahead.

And now, after these many years, I must tell you that all began with you, with your mother. We met for a reason. And that was you. Dear daughter, that was the first time when I cried in front of my Unni. We both melted into you. You sprinkled elixir on our festered wounds. We regarded you as our daughter. The wilted lives at Chittezham rose back to their blooms as you entered here.

Amma revealed everything before Ambika's marriage. But Unni is not like her. He doesn't dare to lose you. That's why he wants us to keep you a secret. Viruthi welcomed you as Unni's daughter. Some believed you were born to him and an orphaned woman somewhere. Unni willingly accepted that version too. Because, to him, his Jyothi was still alive!

Daughter, you were somebody's Vaigai. I knew, one day, you would come to me in search of you; for your own stories. I knew, today you would be reading these. You would have revelations. I speak of no time. No date. No words. Things are abstract sometimes. We might lose ourselves in the game of transforming them into the tangible. If not, let it be behind the pall. Certain things are not to be disclosed. However, if time is to reveal them, we are no one to prevent it. Let things happen. I have rarely spoken to you. I chose not to. It was my decision. Maybe, I wanted it to be so, after my losses. But now, I reconsider. I change.

You have been a seeker. I am pleased that I could satisfy our daughter's eagerness to learn. Your questions are answered here. I speak for those who are not with you, including your mother. And her name, she said, was Senbagam. What you wanted is with the doll. It's yours, daughter.

- Ammoppol

❖ ❖ ❖

15 January 2025

The white ants ate the corners of my attic. The gable louvers were worn and came apart, mantled by cobwebs. No shaft of light could enter the skylight roof tile. It had faded with the fogs of time. I cleared them. I have been the hostage of my fears and insecurities, which were lifted at that very instant. Kodi didn't lie. Instead, I had been a lie; created and nurtured by everyone.

The doll! My hands weren't shaking when I took it from the table. The first ever gift of mine. I felt her. Her golden hair smelled like desiccated earth. I looked at her all over again, fumbling for the thing Ammoppol mentioned.

'The pouch!'

'Charu, our valuables should go in here.'

Kodi always reminded me of this, when we used to play making the cocoa leaf purses.

'The pouch!' The doll had one. I opened it. A small locket tied to a black thread was inside. A pentalloy locket of goddess *Kali*. My sole legacy. The mascot that had been there with the little angel in my father's tale. I couldn't ask anybody why hadn't I come across that earlier. I don't want to know either.

The temple city had a river of people. Yet I happened to them only. As I used to imagine, Ammoppol was indeed a queen! One who fought a real battle. Quite contrary to what I thought, she had been the first one to touch my head. She got me out into this world, and I became my father's little angel. Though I was an uninvited guest, I was never a weed to them. The sight of an old woman taking a baby in her arms came in front of me. The baby looked like a tender dark creeper, fast asleep with a cherubic smile. I could hear her call *'Kunjikkali, our saviour'*, which ended up with her usual laughter.

My journey through their stories prepared me for my reality. The purpose of my existence. There is a future for this soil. And I must be a part. Now I know why I couldn't seek the boon from Him. He wants to give me more than I want. Bonds are not always blood. The child in me is healed. Ms Janah was not wrong.

Yes, I had been a river that took a wrong turn at its origin itself. I met others and reached the convergence. Viruthiyar has been woven deep into the being of Vaigai and to everybody at Chittezham, I have been a river of elixir. I keep them. I carry them along in my depths. And I must flow on... A river named Shadow.

Charulatha Chittezham

❖ ❖ ❖

Charu heaved a sigh after putting the pen down. A bittersweet harmony settled deep in her.

❖ ❖ ❖

CHAPTER 22

THE HOUSE OF DRAGONFLIES

8 March 2028

“The face is missing. It’s a terrific capture! Can I meet the artist?”

It was an old white man who remarked on the portrayal placed in the middle of the hall.

“The woman in the red *sari* is the artist.”

The curator pointed towards the woman standing in the distance. She was gazing at a picture. The canvas captured the eye of a dragonfly that reflected a house.

“Excuse me, hello, it’s a pleasure to meet you, Ms...”

The woman intervened when he floundered.

“I am Charulatha Chittezham. A pleasure to meet you too.”

“Yes. Dear lady, I appreciate your art. Your creations are awesome. Yet, I must say, the female *Oracle* there, eclipses the other pieces. Well, I feel that there is something numinous in the way it’s portrayed. Only she is red. The rest of the pieces are shades of grey... I just wanted the artist to comment on it. May I know?"

He passed an anticipating smile.

"Thank you for your appreciation! Yes. It's more than colours could pour. She is power and could be anybody."

The old man was a French tourist named Gabriel. His freckled face revealed deep-set wrinkles intensified by enthusiasm. There was a young lady with him whose piercing blue eyes floated over the artworks. Both adored art and wanted to know every minute detail of the exhibits in the gallery. With time, more visitors joined them.

Charu walked them to each painting. The ones were showing the river, the laughter of a toothless old woman holding a baby, the grove, the woman with a lantern, the murmuring girls in the attic, *Lord Narasimha* in His spectacular *Kathakali* attire, trees and creepers, a red *bindi* reflecting the surges of love, the man by the green lagoon and many more in rows.

"This young tusker was so naughty. Once, during the temple festival, he had been tied to the huge breadfruit tree. He kept struggling to break the chain and was hurling things around."

Charulatha giggled like a girl as she spoke about the elephant in one of her pieces.

'His mischief is on par with all our children who sleep there.' Achamma's gums were visible as she laughed.

Charu's face suddenly turned sombre.

Spectators moved along with her.

"So, this one makes the title of this exhibition! We just saw it there at the entrance. That sounds marvellous. This piece is poetry to the eyes. I am afraid I shouldn't be asking this. But, does it hold anything special?"

It was the young lady with the man who made the remark. Her slender build leaned in, with curiosity shining in her eyes.

Charu smiled with an unflinching focus on the canvas.

"Yes. That does. You said it's poetry. Rarely do we understand poetry. At times, it is not understood at all. But we get something out of them, don't we? This, too, is the same... But one that is more subjective. There is a place of reassurance, tranquillity, hope, and rejuvenation. It's as pure and gentle as their wings. That's it. And there will be more dragonflies in the coming days. A place encompassing everything. The House of Dragonflies."

A solemn silence settled inside the gallery after the artist's narration.

"Amma..."

All gazes flung towards the corner from where the call came.

"Sorry, my daughter is awake. Thank you all! Have a great time here enjoying these!"

Charu took the toddler from the maid.

❖ ❖ ❖

Stains should be cleared before something new. Last week was spent mending everything like my Chittezham. The house is on the rise. This has been a long wait to see my house transformed. I have been after it for more than three years. Today, I will be back there with my daughter.

My family has given me everything. Life, love, and legacy. I cannot fail them. Due to the linguistic barrier I still couldn't read many letters and newspapers found in Ammoppol's trunk. But those I read, I cannot afford to lose. The person who never spoke to me became someone I hear forever. She speaks to me volumes through what she had left for me. They echo within me even now...

'Daughter, do not feast on poverty when you have in abundance. Don't be a stranger to yourself. Don't ever seek light inside dark chambers. Come out and be the light. Some journeys require walking alone. I can see this calendar in front of me. The last Sunday of this year is laughing at the previous ones in it. And I don't think it is out of joy. It's not... The present is a reminder of the past. Yet, every dawn ignites the promises and hopes of tomorrow, demanding our attention beyond the confines of today.'

My heart abounds with emotions. Each face I remember gratefully.

I received a call from Kodi yesterday. I wanted to share information about the House of Dragonflies, and she had some exciting news for me as well. Her daughter, Amutha, has secured a private job, and they both live together now.

Last week, I called and spoke to Agavan's wife, Poovizhi. I was relieved to hear from her. There has been a gradual improvement in Agavan. He has started using walkers. The challenges have helped the couple find a new sense of bonding between them.

My love for him cannot dwindle. I am thankful to him. He is the reason why I got my Kodi. He is the reason I was able to move this far. He will still sweeten my cup of emotions. Love is not sticking to somebody. It transcends. It frees. He will always be protected, and so will his loved ones.

Bonds are not always blood.

❖ ❖ ❖

The car crossed the bridge. The radiant afternoon kept floating in Viruthiyaru. The house stood like a mother draped in *mundu* and *veshti*. Workers had already left the premises. This time, Charulatha entered Chittezham not to abandon it but to embrace it. She has mended it to transform to welcome more dragonflies.

Her stare got hooked up to the attic for a while.

'Somebody inside the attic must still be watching me!'

Charu embraced a mystical silence.

"This is my daughter, our daughter, Paru. Welcome home, darling!"

Charu kissed the girl who started prattling to her by then.

She took out the sapling from the car and walked towards the southwest of Chittezham. The well had been cleaned. The land was barren there. No sprouting had ever come out of the dead mother breadfruit tree. She planted it and watered it. The soil will continue to spread its branches further.

A month later, on April 10, 2028, Chittezham will be 'the House of Dragonflies', welcoming the unwanted and orphaned children, the first one now on her shoulder.

The words resonated within her.

'...They visit the purest places. Haven't you watched dragonflies near the tree by the well? Our blood sleeps there. There are plenty of them. That's why I tell you, even after their time is over here, our loved ones will stay back with us.'

"Amma... "

She silently heeded and headed to a dry wind that came forth to kiss her, from a far-off land that once bore more flowers than girls.

A flight of dragonflies hovered over her.

❖ ❖ ❖

GLOSSARY

Kavu - Traditional name given to the sacred groves

Kali - Goddess Kali

Onam - The annual festival of harvest celebrated by the people of Kerala

Tharavad - Ancestral home

Marumakkathayam - The system in Nair Tharavad where matriarchy has been practised. The girl born in the family would be given a higher role and power.

Karanavar - The head of the family

Karkkadakam - The last month of the Malayalam year, known for heavy rainfall

Thulam - The third month in the Malayalam calendar

Irikkappindam - The peculiar custom in which, ritually, a person is declared dead while alive. The person thus faces complete eviction from a place.

Mundu and Veshti - Traditional attire of Malayali women

Bhagavathi - Goddess

Para daivangal - Divine deities of the house

Kavalappara Komban - A tusker, infamous for his wrathful nature, who belonged to the early 20th Century

Nair, Namboothiri and Pandara - Different Hindu Castes

Sage Parasuram - The sixth incarnation among the Dashavatara of the preserver god Vishnu in Hinduism

Mana - The residence of Namboothiris / Kerala Brahmins

Raukka - Blouse

Sloka - A couplet of Sanskrit verse

Thiruvathirakkali - One traditional group dance form of Malayali women

Chovva dosham - Astrological finding in one's horoscope, as per the planet Mars' influence on the person

Machchu - Traditional attic

Vishu - A Hindu festival marking the beginning of an astronomical year

Vishukkani - The first sight of fullness and prosperity seen at dawn, on the day of Vishu

Vishukkaineettam - The first monetary offering made by the older members to the younger ones, auspiciously during the season of Vishu.

Davani - A simple outfit worn by young girls in South India

Kindi - One of the holy vessels used for doing poojas and rituals

Thamburatti/Thambratti - A respectful form of address for a woman, especially one belonging to an upper caste

Kathakali - A classical dance-drama art form of Kerala

Narasimha Murti - The fourth incarnation of Lord Vishnu

Prahlada charitham - The story of Prahlada, an Asura king in the Hindu scriptures who was an ardent devotee of Lord Vishnu

Vyloppilli Sreedhara Menon's* poem *Mambazham - A famous poem in Malayalam portrays a mother mourning the loss of her son.

Vijayadasami - The Dussehra festival